I0575982

merry little bookshop

A CHRISTMAS & HANUKKAH NOVELLA

ALI BRADY

Copyright © 2025 by Alison Hammer and Bradeigh Godfrey

All rights reserved.

No part of this book may be reproduced in any form or by any electronic or mechanical means, including information storage and retrieval systems, without written permission from the author, except for the use of brief quotations in a book review.

ALSO BY ALI BRADY

NOVELS

The Beach Trap

The Comeback Summer

Until Next Summer

Battle of the Bookstores

———

NOVELLA

One Night, Two Holidays

For anyone who's ever felt like they don't belong:
May your shelves overflow with stories,
your holidays sparkle with magic,
and your life be filled with people
who make you feel at home.

CHAPTER 1

SHIRA

28 DAYS UNTIL I CAN LEAVE

Nothing says Thanksgiving dinner like three steak tacos and a side of guacamole. To-go.

I know I should be thankful that *anything* in this tiny Texas town is open on Thanksgiving, but that's a lot to ask of a girl who is alone in the world—or at least the state—on a holiday that's defined by homestyle cooking and, well, home.

Not that I have a "home" in the sentimental meaning of the word. My studio apartment back in Chicago is about as homey as a shoebox, and my parents sold the house I grew up in years ago, trading it—and each other—for newer models. When I told them I wouldn't be around for Thanksgiving this year, neither seemed to mind much. To them, my absence probably feels like every other year when I do the kids-of-divorced-parents shuffle, trading off between families.

Except this year, I'm not with either of them because I didn't have the balls to tell my boss no when he presented me with this "great opportunity" to get "on the ground experience" running one of the temporary pop-up shops we place in properties across the country.

So here I am, sitting in a hard plastic chair at a taqueria that smells like sizzling meat and fresh corn tortillas, my stomach growling as I wait. The older woman who took my order has disappeared back into the kitchen, where she's bickering in Spanish with a man I assume is her husband. Even though I barely understand one in every ten words, I can tell their argument is playful and spirited. It makes me yearn for the kind of home I never had but always wanted.

Before I can get too wistful about a childhood that wasn't all that idyllic, my phone buzzes with another text in our group chat. Maya, my best friend and college roommate, has been sending meme after meme to try and lift my spirits. This one features a giant turkey, strutting her stuff, with the caption: *You only want me for my breasts!*

I laugh and shake my head, grateful for the long-distance support. I should have taken Maya up on the offer to come along and help get everything set up since she had the week off from teaching third grade. Turns out I greatly underestimated the amount of work it would take to turn a blank space into a bookshop—even a small one. And how lonely it would feel.

"lol. I like big breasts, and I cannot lie," Naomi texts back. She's in Vermont for the week, visiting her girlfriend Rachel's family.

"Miss you bitches," Talia texts. She's in Miami with her parents and grandparents, but unlike me, she'll be back home in Chicago by Sunday night. *"Remind me not to eat for the next week."*

This is followed by a photo of the spread at her Thanksgiving dinner: turkey and stuffing, mashed potatoes, green beans, and at least six different types of dessert. My mouth waters just looking at it.

"Want to see my Thanksgiving dinner options?" I text, then send a photo of the taqueria: bright pink walls, fluttering paper

flags hanging from the ceiling, and a hand-written chalkboard menu.

"*On any other day that would look amazing,*" Maya replies. "*But today: Fuck Conor.*"

"*Fuck Conor,*" Talia agrees.

"*Fuck him to hell and back,*" Naomi adds.

I sigh as I text back: "*As long as he gives me the promotion when this is all over, I'll be happy.*"

"*If he doesn't, we swap his protein powder for a laxative!!!*" Talia replies.

"*YES! Perfect for the world's shittiest boss,*" Maya adds, followed by a string of crying-while-laughing and poop emojis.

"*Or maybe something that wouldn't come with a string of torts and possible criminal charges?*" Naomi offers, showing off her law degree.

Smiling, I shake my head. These girls have been my "ride or die" since we met at Hillel freshman year at Indiana University, and they hate my boss as much, if not more, than I do.

It would have been flattering when Conor said I was "perfect for this job" if it had *anything* to do with my performance or my potential. But the truth is, I'd be going in for second helpings of my mom's famous stuffing if my name were Molly Quinn or Christina Wallace.

But alas, my name is Shira Schwartz.

When Conor suggested I wouldn't mind being away for the entire month of December since I don't celebrate Christmas, I could have reminded him that I *do* celebrate Hanukkah—but that's not the "can-do" attitude he wants to see for me to finally get the promotion he's been dangling over my head for the last year and a half.

Plus, it goes against the philosophy that's gotten me this far at work and in life—trying to focus attention on the things I have in common with whatever group I'm in and not on all the ways I'm different.

But I am different than the "bros" at work. Which is why I'm here, waiting for take-out to bring back to the old textile mill that's being turned into a month-long Christmas market. When the doors open tomorrow for Black Friday, it'll be filled with holiday cheer and a variety of shops, including "The Book Nook," the pop-up bookshop my company is currently managing temporary locations of in thirteen different states.

Normally, my job involves conducting a cost-benefit analysis of the city where we're considering a pop-up shop, including the demographics, competition, and available real estate. If all systems are a go, then we have a team of managers across the country who hire and train the temporary staff.

But this location, in a small town about fifty miles west of Dallas, wasn't planned. It's a last-minute favor for one of Conor's business school bros, and since all our managers in the Texas-Oklahoma region were already assigned to other pop-ups, I got the "opportunity."

Lucky me.

"Hey, Shir - You know what would make your month in Texas go by faster?" Talia texts.

"A time machine?" I reply, though I'm pretty sure I already know what she's going to say.

"A holiday hookup!" she replies.

The other girls chime in with their agreement, sending GIFs of sexy Santas, sexy cowboys, sexy...reindeer?

"Yeah, because that's soooo me," I reply, laughing. I'm not a forever flirt like Talia, who chases pleasure with a rotating list of men, and I don't swipe the apps searching for a husband like Maya. As with most things, I fall somewhere in the middle. The girls think I'm shy and reserved, but really, I just like to have an emotional connection with a guy before I fully bare myself.

"So don't be you." Maya texts back. *"It could be fun to channel someone else for a month."*

I'm searching for the perfect GIF to reply with—someone wearing those silly glasses with a fake nose and mustache—when the front door opens, jingling the bells above it.

"Jonny!" the woman behind the counter says. "What a sight for sore eyes."

I look up to see for myself, and I couldn't agree more. The man is tall and sturdy, just like the kind of boys you'd imagine they breed in Texas. He's got his back to me, so I'm free to let my eyes linger, appreciating the way he fills out his dark blue jeans. His brown leather work boots look worn, as if they're used for actual work and not a fashion statement, unlike the guys in Chicago. The red flannel shirt that covers his broad shoulders looks so soft that I want to rub my cheek against the fabric.

On impulse, I take a quick photo and send it to the group chat, with the message: *Look what just walked in.*

"Hey, Rosa." His voice is low, with a hint of a Texas drawl. It sounds like graveled honey, and suddenly, I understand the appeal. "Mama sent me over with a plate for you and Miguel."

My phone buzzes again, and both Rosa and the handsome cowboy turn to look at me. My cheeks instantly go hot, and I put my phone face down, even though there's no way he could know I just sent a photo of his ass to my friends across the country. I watch as his blue eyes travel the length of me, taking me in the way I'd done moments before to him.

He looks to be about my age, maybe a little older. Early thirties? His hair color is somewhere between dark blond and light brown, and it looks messy but styled, like he spent time on it but doesn't want it to look like he did. He's got a five o'clock shadow hiding an almost boyish face—but the way he's looking at me is anything but innocent. This is the kind of man they write country songs about, the ones who are up to no good and fun to get into a little bit of trouble with.

Not that I would. Get in trouble. Despite what my friends want me to do, I'm here for work. To get in, get out, and make a good enough impression that I'll get promoted and finally feel like my life is going somewhere.

Except now my phone is blowing up, and when I sneak a glance at it, I see why:

Talia: Gurrl, go for it. HAVE FUN.

Maya: Cosign. You don't have to marry the guy.

Talia: But you can bang him!

Naomi: Ride that cowboy!

My cheeks grow even hotter as I look up. The cowboy flashes me an easy grin and says, "If I knew there'd be such a pretty customer here, I would've brought you a plate, too. Or at least a piece of pie. Are you an apple or a pumpkin lover?"

My mouth waters, and not just because I really could go for a slice of apple or pumpkin pie. Hell, I'd even settle for pecan.

"Flirt, flirt, flirt!" Talia chants in my head.

"Sorry," I say, finding my voice. Rather, an impersonation of Talia's voice. "But you're going to have to work a little harder than that to find out what kind of lover I am."

His eyes flicker with surprise and amusement, like he didn't expect that response—but he likes it.

"Noted," he says, his eyes dipping back down my body. My stomach flips. No wonder Talia's always smiling; this is fun. Thrilling.

"You leave her alone," Rosa says, coming back around the counter. "This sweet girl doesn't need your kind of trouble."

"Aw, come on, darlin'," he says to her. "You know I've only got eyes for you."

"Shoo." She has to reach up to slap his shoulder playfully. "You get out of here and tell your Mama we said thank you."

"Happy Thanksgiving," he says, bending to kiss her on the cheek. She shakes her head and goes back to the kitchen, but it's clear from her smile that she loves both the attention and the troublemaker.

He turns to me, his eyes zeroing in on my face in a way that makes my spine straighten. "See you around," he says, giving me a tip of his imaginary hat before adding, "I hope."

The door opens, and he's gone before I can muster the nerve to ask for his number or give him mine.

"Sarah?" a voice says.

I lean back in the chair and look back at my phone; there have to be at least thirty new messages.

"Sarah?"

I look up. Rosa is standing in front of me, holding out a paper bag with my food.

"Oh! Yes, sorry." I forgot that I gave her my generic "Starbucks" name. No one raises an eyebrow and asks a Sarah what kind of name that is or where she's *really* from or what, if any, god she believes in. And they don't make lame jokes about "She-Ra, Princess of Power." Sarahs can fit in anywhere; they can belong no matter who or where they are.

"Thank you so much!" I say, smiling. "Really, I'm so glad you were open today, otherwise I may have starved!"

Taking the bag, I stand, surprised by how stiff my muscles are after a single day of manual labor. I walk outside just in time to see the cowboy pull away in his very big, very Texas truck.

For one split second, I consider an alternate universe where I walked out to find him waiting for me. He'd tell me to "hop in, darlin,'" then take me home to meet his family. After a delicious homemade turkey dinner (tacos, be damned!), he would take me back to the market where he'd help me unpack all the boxes and organize books on the shelves I spent all day putting

7

together—even though I didn't have the "another adult human," the instructions called for.

But this is real life, not one of the romance novels I'll be selling to the ladies of Azalea, Texas. I sigh, then get into my rental car—an embarrassing bright green Nissan Cube—and head back to the store to finish getting ready.

Because tomorrow, the market opens, and I'll be one step closer to Christmas morning when I'll fly home to Chicago to spend the day with my girlfriends like we always do.

It's my year to pick the movie we'll be watching along with our traditional Jewish Christmas dinner of takeout Chinese food. I'm planning a double header: *The Wizard of Oz*, because there really is no place like home, and *Love, Actually*, because it's objectively the best Christmas movie ever. Plus, it celebrates platonic love along with the romantic kind, which feels right. My girlfriends are the loves of my life, my true family, the only people in the world I can be my real self around—and I can't wait to get back to them.

It's going to be the longest December ever, but if I can make it through, I'll be back where I belong.

CHAPTER 2

JONNY

27 DAYS UNTIL THE BEST DAY OF THE YEAR!

Coming home always feels like slipping on an old pair of boots I haven't worn in years—comfortable and broken-in, every mark and crease familiar, yet something about them doesn't feel like mine anymore. I hurry down the stairs, following the scent of biscuits and gravy toward the kitchen, but I hesitate at the threshold, listening to the laughter and conversation inside. Caught, as always, between the tug of belonging and the urge to stand apart.

But then my dad spots me in the doorway.

"Look who decided to join the land of the living!" he booms, the same line he tossed at me practically every morning of my teenage years. Usually, Dad would be helping Mom with breakfast, but this year he's stretched out in a recliner, healing from surgery.

"It's nine a.m. the day after Thanksgiving, old man," I tell him, grinning as I enter the crowded kitchen. "Most people are probably still in bed."

"Most people are lazy bums." That's from my older brother, Isaac. He's sitting at the big farmhouse table with everyone else, feeding leftover apple pie to his youngest in the highchair, complete with airplane zooming noises.

"Compared to you, that's true," his wife Annabel chimes in, which is exactly why he's the heir to my dad's alfalfa farm.

"Need I remind you," Isaac says to me, "that the workday starts at dawn? Farms don't run on a nine-to-five."

Everyone at the table chuckles. I'm about to fire back that neither do any of the businesses I've built from scratch, that I know plenty about early mornings, late nights, and constant worry. But I stop myself. No point in explaining when it'd just lead to more ribbing about what constitutes "real work" and how my "fancy degrees" and "soft hands" disqualify me from it.

"Jonathan James," Mom calls from the stove, "you better get over here and give me a kiss."

I obey, coming closer and pressing a kiss to the top of her head. As I do, I grab a wooden spoon so I can sneak a quick taste of the gravy she's stirring. Before she can scold me, I say, "Need me to drop anything off at Kara and Kyle's on my way into town?"

It works; Mom smiles and nods at a foil-covered dish on the counter. "That'd be lovely, sweetheart. Thank you."

My younger sister is on bed rest for a high-risk pregnancy, due in three months. Her doctor agreed that she could attend yesterday's Thanksgiving dinner, as long as she spent the rest of the weekend resting.

"Pull up a chair and stay awhile, son," Dad says, but I'm already shrugging on the tan Carhartt work jacket I've had since high school.

"Can't," I say, shaking my head. "Not after being told every damn day of my life to stop burning daylight."

"Language," my older sister Bianca scolds, eying my nieces and nephews sitting around the table. Her husband Chad bites back a grin; Bianca used to swear like a sailor before becoming a mom.

"If we're not supposed to say damn, why's it in the Bible?" I wink at my oldest nephew, who's staring at me wide-eyed. "I need to check on the space for the holiday market, see how it's coming along."

"Oh, that can wait 'til tomorrow," Dad says, rubbing a hand over his salt-and-pepper beard. "The day after Thanksgiving's not for shopping, it's for—"

"Leftovers and football, like God intended," Isaac and Bianca finish in unison, and everyone laughs. That launches a discussion about the Cowboys' win yesterday, and how the Aggies better show up today.

"I'll be back before kickoff," I tell them, "but speaking of leftovers..." I reach across the table and swipe a slice of pumpkin pie with my bare hand.

Bianca swats me. "Jonny! Get yourself a plate."

In response, I grin and take a massive bite of the pie.

Then I go around the table and give a little greeting to each of my six nieces and nephews: fist-bumps, nose-boops, a tickle under the chin for baby Nellie. Even our golden retrievers, Samson and Delilah, get a scratch behind the ears.

After that, I snag the keys to Dad's truck, stuff the rest of the pumpkin pie in my mouth, take the foil-covered dish from my mom, and head out the door.

I point Dad's F-350 toward town, following the road cutting through winter-brown alfalfa fields under a cloudy sky. Soon I'm passing Henderson's Hardware with its faded sign, the diner that I'm sure still smells like burnt coffee, the squat little high school where we all spent Friday nights under the lights

It's not a cute, picturesque small town—it's a tired place where nothing's really changed in decades. Other than a few more boarded-up shops on Main Street and the paint on the water tower fading, it's the same as when I grew up. Which is comforting, sure, but also why I vowed never to get stuck here. The past few years, I've been all about innovation, pushing the envelope, chasing growth, and being here is a reminder of why I left. People here just aren't interested in that. Especially when it comes to me.

After swinging by my little sister's house to drop off the food—her husband meets me at the door and whispers that she's sleeping—I head further into town. Soon I'm pulling into the cracked asphalt parking lot of the old textile mill, its brick walls still stamped with the faded outline of a long-gone sign. The site of this year's Azalea Christmas Market.

For two decades, the market has been a town tradition, started by Dad when he was mayor, to keep Azalea's holiday spending local. But this year, a tractor accident left him with a broken left hip and a right ankle fractured in three places, so he's had to hand over the reins. Kara would do a great job, but with the high-risk pregnancy, she's out. Isaac's busy with winter duties around the farm, Bianca's got her hands full with three kids, and Mom's nursing Dad back to health.

So, it's on me. Which is why I'm back for my longest visit ever since hightailing it out of here for college twelve years ago. I *always* come for Thanksgiving and Christmas—Christmas is my favorite holiday, and Thanksgiving is a close second—but I never stay longer than a couple of days. Got to escape before this place sucks me back in.

It'd be too dramatic to call myself the prodigal son or black sheep, but as the only McKay who doesn't still live in Azalea, I might as well have a big neon sign over my head that says ONE OF THESE THINGS IS NOT LIKE THE OTHERS.

When I step out of the truck, the cool air carries that ever-present tang of manure. I grab Dad's tool belt from the back of the truck and buckle it around my hips, figuring I'll tighten up that squeaky door I noticed yesterday. Then I shove my hands in my jacket pockets and head into the building, whistling "I'll Be Home for Christmas."

Even though it's not exactly my ideal scenario, spending a month sleeping in my childhood bed and being harassed by my siblings at every turn (nor am I thrilled to be back in a town where everyone remembers exactly how much of a pain in the ass I was as a kid), there's always something nice about being home for the holidays.

And honestly? I'm excited about my plans for the Christmas market.

Dad always crammed it all into a drafty old barn, but I convinced him to let me try something different. The textile building is half-renovated and rough around the edges, but I had a vision: the old foreman's office and other storage rooms are perfect for small shops, and booths all across the production floor will sell everything from handmade quilts to cowboy boots and hats, beeswax candles, jars of local honey, and toys for the kids.

Same stuff that's sold every year. Except this time, I'm trying something new: a pop-up bookstore as the main attraction. My buddy from grad school owns a company that runs these, and he did me a solid and helped pull this all together in record time.

When I step inside, the lights are off, and the air smells faintly of dust and old grease. My boots echo on the concrete as I round a corner—and collide with someone holding a box.

A big box, teetering dangerously.

"Whoa there," I say, steadying the box with one hand.

I glance around it, expecting to see someone from town,

here to set up their shop. Instead, I see the face of a stranger: full lips, parted in surprise, and glossy dark hair with swooping bangs over the biggest brown eyes I've ever seen.

Well, not a stranger exactly.

"Oh, hey, taco girl," I say, grinning.

Color rushes to her cheeks. "I—uh—hi."

"Allow me." I slide the box out of her arms before she can argue. It's heavier than expected, and when I peek inside the open flap, I see why. Books.

And then it clicks: Conor said he was sending someone to run the pop-up bookshop, although I had imagined a middle-aged librarian type. Certainly not...her. Barely five foot something with curves for days, wearing jeans and a sweater that fit like they were stitched with her in mind.

I'm kind of a sucker for a woman in a sweater, and this one —V-neck, form-fitting, a soft camel color...yeah. This one's working its magic.

"You're setting up the bookshop?" I say, forcing my gaze up to meet her eyes.

"I finished last night," she says. "Wanted to be ready for all the Black Friday shoppers."

We both look around the vacant space.

"Sorry, guess you didn't get the memo," I say, feeling genuinely bad about that—but I swear I told Conor. "The market starts on Saturday. Black Friday's not really a thing here, but we'll have a good crowd tomorrow."

She tucks a strand of hair behind her ear, eyes darting to the tool belt at my waist. "Well, in that case, are you—um, do you have a minute to help me with something? I put together all the bookshelves yesterday, but two are still kind of wobbly, and I'm afraid if I put any books on them, the whole thing's going to—"

"Slow down, darlin'." I flash her an easy smile. "We're not in a rush."

I know I'm laying it on a little thick, the whole small-town charm routine—but the way she flushes and smiles? Worth it.

"Sorry," she breathes.

"Your boss is the one who should be sorry." And I'll be giving Conor shit about it as soon as I get a chance. "Sending you here all by yourself to haul heavy boxes and build shelves? What was he thinking?"

She lets out a half-laugh. "Not sure he cares."

"Sounds like I need to kick his ass, then."

"Please don't," she says, sighing. Then, in a quieter voice, "I really need this job to go well."

My joke about kicking Conor's ass doesn't feel so jokey anymore. How could he expect her to get all this set up alone?

"I'm Jonny, by the way." I can't shake her hand, given the box in my arms, so I just nod. "Jonny McKay."

Her mouth twitches. "Of course that's your name," she mumbles.

"And what's that supposed to mean?"

"Oh, nothing." She shakes her head, cheeks flushing an even deeper pink. *Very pretty.*

It makes me want to tease her a little more. "No, no, you have an opinion about my name. Out with it."

"Just seems a fitting name for..." She waves a hand in my direction. "All this."

"All what?" I raise an eyebrow, but I don't mind the way her eyes are lingering on me. Not at all. When she doesn't answer, I say, "Now here's the part where you tell me *your* name."

"Oh..." She hesitates. "It's, um. Sarah."

"Just Sarah? No last name?"

"You walked in off the street," she says, lifting her chin. "How do I know I can trust you with that information?"

I nod seriously. "Never can tell what kind of riffraff is gonna help you carry boxes and fix wobbly shelves."

She immediately reaches for the box. "Sorry, I don't mean to be all lady-in-distress. If you're too busy—"

"Ladies in distress are my specialty." I grin, hefting the box higher. "I've got this. Lead the way."

CHAPTER 3

SHIRA

27 DAYS UNTIL I CAN LEAVE

How is it that one little "darlin'" can turn me—a relatively strong and independent woman—into some sort of damsel who not only agrees to have a big, strong, handsome man come to her rescue, but actually wants it?

Especially a man like *this*: toolbelt slung low on his hips, scuffed work boots, worn jeans, unshaven jaw, looking like he just rolled out of bed. Totally not my type. At all.

"Wow," Jonny says when we step through the door. "It looks like a real bookstore."

"It does, doesn't it?"

This makes Jonny chuckle, but I put in too much blood, sweat, and tears—literally—not to take credit where credit is due. And the bookstore does look good—white bookcases line the industrial brick walls on both sides, and all but the two wobbly ones are stocked with colorful books, organized by genre.

I arranged a few small tables in the middle to encourage browsing and help direct the flow of traffic. One features a flat lay of books that are currently on the bestseller list, another has books by authors local to Texas, and a third features bookish swag and accessories that are perfect for stocking stuffers.

And my favorite part: against the wall of windows, I created a small children's section with shorter, wider shelves, and stuffed animals inspired by characters from popular picture and chapter books. It's just missing something soft and cozy, like a colorful rug, so kids don't have to sit on the cold, concrete floor to flip through books while their parents shop.

"It looks incredible," Jonny says, and it sounds like he really means it. Then he smirks at me and adds, "But...is it normal for all the top shelves to be empty? Is that some bold new design trend I'm not aware of?"

My cheeks flush. "I ordered a stepladder, but it's going to take three to five business days to get here."

Same-day delivery and the ability to have anything from sushi to Starbucks dropped off right at my door are the number one and number two things I'm currently missing most about Chicago, after my friends, of course.

They're going to lose their shit when I tell them I ran into the hottie from the taco place and that he works at the Christmas Market, too. It's like a real Hanukkah miracle, Texas style.

"Good thing I'm here, then," Jonny says, smiling. "I'm happy to be your designated top-shelf-reacher, after I fix those shelves."

He walks over and puts a hand on one of the empty shelves, giving it a gentle shake. "Yep. Definitely wobbles."

"Did you think I was lying to get you alone in here?" I ask, pulling the wrinkled instruction sheet from my pocket. "I followed all the cartoon pictures, but those little locky-spinny pieces aren't easy to tighten."

He grins. "The Cam locks?"

"If you say so." I reach into my pocket and pull out a quarter. "Here."

Jonny's lips twitch as he stares at the coin. "I'm not sure if I should be offended that you're trying to pay me or hurt that you think I'm worth that little."

I roll my eyes the way I imagine Talia would. "It's to tighten the locky-spinny pieces."

"Cam locks," he repeats, eyes twinkling. Then he whistles softly as he looks over all the other shelves. "You used a quarter to tighten all these? Girl, those pretty little fingers of yours must be *aching*."

My stomach flutters. Somehow, he made that sound exceptionally dirty. And I think I like it. "Well, yeah," I admit, flustered.

His grin widens, like he's well aware of the effect he's having on me, and probably most women in a hundred-mile radius. "Allow me to introduce you to a little thing called a flathead screwdriver," he says, pulling one from his tool belt.

"See, if you'd offered me that yesterday instead of pie, we could've gotten somewhere."

"Touché," Jonny says. "I could make a joke about calling me the next time you need a good screw, but I won't—because I'm a gentleman."

A laugh bursts out of me. "Sure, you are."

He smiles, revealing his dimples. He's clearly having fun with this, too. I flash back to the older woman's warning last night. She's right—Shira Schwartz doesn't need Jonny McKay's kind of trouble. But like Maya said, it could be fun to channel someone else for a month.

My whole life, I've gone for the sweet, nerdy, Jewish guys my parents expected me to be with. Men from good families who have promising careers with robust 401(k)s, and who are respectful, almost to a fault. The last guy I dated asked permission before he did every little thing in bed: *May I lick your nipple? Is it okay if I add another finger?*

A guy with this cocky confidence would definitely be different. Shira wouldn't be into it, but maybe "Sarah" would enjoy it? Even get off on it? Like the girls keep reminding me—this month could go a lot faster if I let myself have some fun. And Jonny seems like the kind of guy it would be easy to have some fun with.

It takes him less than two minutes to deconstruct the shelf that took me forty-five minutes to build, and about five minutes to put it back together. The second one goes down and up just as fast, and I wish there were more manual labor tasks I could get his help with.

Jonny doesn't seem in a rush to leave either, because he moves over to one of the shelves I already filled with books and gives it a little shake. "Not bad," he says, when it doesn't budge. "I'm impressed you did this all by yourself."

I straighten my shoulders and stand as tall as a five-foot-two woman in tennis shoes can. "What can I say? I'm tougher than I look."

"You look pretty tough to me," he says, that slight drawl sending a chill up and down my spine. "I mean pretty, comma, and tough."

Oh. My. God. Grammar has never been so hot.

"Uh, thanks," I say, forgetting for a second that I'm supposed to be channeling Talia and her flirtatious confidence. "I mean, I'm glad you were here. I'm pretty lucky the market has such a handsome handyman on the job."

Jonny's lips draw tight, just for a moment, and I hope I didn't offend him. Is there a more PC title for someone who wears a tool belt and fixes things that are broken?

"I really do appreciate the help," I say, trying to bring his smile back.

It works; that crooked grin reappears. "Well, I live to serve. Want some help filling these shelves? Now that they're sturdy enough to handle it?"

I hesitate, wishing it were any section other than romance that needs to be stocked. I am not skilled enough to handle casual get-to-know-you banter over bodice rippers. "Oh, I'm sure you have more important things to do."

"The only other thing on my list is fixing a squeaky door," he says, leaning against the bookshelf like he has no intention of going anywhere. "And maybe I'd like to hang out with a pretty bookseller for a while longer."

A thrill runs through me, but I try not to let it show on my face. Flirting with Jonny is dangerously fun. Can I actually do this? Have a holiday fling with a hot handyman?

The girls are going to lose their minds.

"In that case, we can start with these," I say, moving toward a stack of contemporary romance novels with deceptively innocent cartoon covers.

The first few are already in alphabetical order, so I hand them to Jonny, then work to get the next stack ready.

"How long have you been a bookseller?" he asks.

"Honestly?"

"My mama says that's the best policy," he says, flashing me a smile that reveals two deep dimples beneath the few days' stubble on his cheeks.

"Well, then, this is officially my second day," I tell him. "I work for the company that places pop-up shops like this in empty storefronts, but I'm usually on the back end."

"Then how'd you end up down here in Nowhereville, Texas, for the holidays?" he asks. "Lose a bet? Draw the short straw?"

"Long story." I bring my hand to my chest, where my Star of David necklace is hidden under my sweater. "But I've been an avid reader my whole life, so it's not the worst thing."

The words ring true, and I'm surprised to realize that I'm not as miserable as I thought I would be. The last two days have been really hard, and muscles I didn't even know I had are aching, but there's something rewarding about seeing the physical results of my labor grow around me.

And the more the bookstore has come together, the more excited I am about helping people find their next favorite book. Much to my parents' chagrin, I've always loved losing myself in fictional worlds—which is kind of what I'm doing here.

Plus, being in Azalea means I'm not stuck in the office, pretending to care how the Bears did last weekend or that Conor's jokes are funny instead of vaguely offensive. That's probably the biggest perk of all.

I can hear Talia's voice in my head, "*Except maybe for a no-strings holiday hookup with the handyman...*"

My cheeks warm at the thought, and I let my eyes linger on Jonny's backside, wondering if I could really sleep with a man I know next to nothing about. Who knows nothing about me. Not even my real name.

We could be getting to know each other now. I search for something we can talk about, then glance at the book in my hand.

"Do you read?" I blurt.

Jonny looks down at me, then at the M/M cowboy romance I'm handing him to add to the shelf. His eyebrows lift.

"I don't mean *can* you read," I say quickly. "Of course you can read. I mean, *do* you read? Books. For fun?" *Stop talking, Shira!*

He chuckles. "I can read just fine. As far as whether or not I do read..." Something dings in his pocket, and he fishes it out, mouthing, "Sorry," before answering.

"Yes, my dear?" He listens and nods, offering an occasional "Mmm hmm" to whoever he's talking to.

22

I continue stacking ACOTAR books in the correct order and try not to listen, but Jonny doesn't seem to care—he doesn't move away or lower his voice.

"No, no, it's okay," he says. "I'm at your beck and call until this baby comes."

Baby?

I glance down at his left hand; no ring. Not that that means anything these days. Still, I can't help but be a tiny bit disappointed. "Sarah" might be more adventurous than Shira, but she would never hook up with a man who's about to have a baby with another woman. The girls won't fault me for that.

I keep listening.

"If you're craving dilly beans, then I'll stop by and grab some on my way home after I—okay, I'll grab them now." He shakes his head, a fond smile tugging at his lips, then ends the call.

"I've got to run," he says to me. "But I can come back later? In about an hour?"

"No," I say, too sharp. He blinks, surprised. And even though it's a complete sentence, I keep rambling. "I'll probably be done by then."

His eyebrows draw together. "Okay...well, in that case, what are you doing tonight? I could give you a tour of the town. Take you to dinner?"

A few minutes ago, this would've felt like a win—*he asked me out!*—but now, all that fluttery excitement has sunk straight to the pit of my stomach.

"I'm afraid I can't," I say. "But thank you again for your help."

Jonny's staring at me like I'm the pages of a book he wants to read, but it's written in a foreign language. As much as I'd love to translate it all for him, I turn and busy myself with organizing the rest of the books.

He doesn't say anything else, and a moment later, I hear his boots echo as he walks out the door, going home to bring whatever dilly beans are to his baby mama.

It's probably for the best. As much as I loved the idea of trying on a braver, bolder, more forward version of myself, that's not why I'm here. I've worked too hard for this promotion; the last thing I need is a distraction—especially one who looks that good in a pair of jeans.

But it would have been fun...

CHAPTER 4

JONNY

24 DAYS UNTIL THE BEST DAY OF THE YEAR

The best thing about being the Fun Single Uncle™ is that I get to pull stunts my older siblings (responsible parents, rule followers, blah blah blah) would never attempt.

Case in point: rolling up to the elementary school on a Monday afternoon, signing out my oldest niece and nephew like I'm on a covert op, and whisking them away for an exclusive Uncle Jonny Special Activity. The mission? Have a ridiculous amount of fun, secure their eternal devotion, and then dump them back on their parents a couple of hours later—overstimulated, hopped up on sugar, and believing I'm cooler than Santa.

"Who's excited to see the Christmas market?" I ask, looking in the rearview mirror.

Two voices from the back seat of the truck shout in unison, "Meeeeee!"

"Y'all are gonna love it," I say, grinning. "There's a sweet shop—"

"Yay!" they cheer.

"—and lots of toys—"

More cheers.

"And..." I lower my voice dramatically. "There's even a bookstore."

Silence.

Two pairs of eyes blink at me from the rear-view mirror. Six-year-old Maggie (Bianca's oldest) looks politely confused. Seven-year-old Jake (Isaac's oldest) looks like I just suggested we get a cavity filled for fun.

I shouldn't be surprised, but I can't help the tiny pang of disappointment at their reactions. I mean, I get it. Azalea has never had a bookstore, and the McKays aren't a big reading family. Growing up, the only books I'd ever laid hands on came from the sad little school library. It wasn't until college, when I stumbled into an indie bookstore searching for a restroom, that I realized there were entire stores *just for books*. My mind was blown. Ever since, I've found a favorite bookstore in every city I've called home. There's something about them that makes the world feel bigger—a reminder of how much I don't know and how much I still want to learn.

That's exactly why I'm excited about the pop-up bookstore: the chance to open the eyes of people here in town to a bigger, wider world. Especially the kids. And *especially* my own nieces and nephews.

I reach the old textile mill and pull into the parking lot. It's about half full, not bad for the first day of December, especially at a new location. But if it doesn't get busier as the month goes on...well, let's just say everyone will know who to blame: the guy who spent his teenage years raising hell, then bolted for the city at the first chance he got.

Shaking that off, I refocus on my niece and nephew.

"If y'all are good for me at the market," I say, turning in my seat, "I'll buy you whatever book you want."

Jake narrows his eyes in a way that reminds me of my older brother, like he's analyzing the market value of this offer.

"Only if you get me something at the sweet shop first," he says.

I sigh. "Deal."

Inside, the place isn't packed, but it isn't a ghost town either. I lead Jake and Maggie through the maze of shops and booths, waving and greeting people as we pass. We grab a couple jars of spiced apple preserves for my mom, and, of course, more of those damn dilly beans Kara's been craving.

Next up, the sweet shop. I buy each kid a giant lollipop, the kind my mom never let me have because they're just going to end up half-eaten and covered in pocket lint.

Not my problem, though. I'm just the cool uncle.

Then we make our way back to the entrance, where the bookstore sits in the old front office and counting room. Only a handful of people are browsing the shelves, but at least it's not empty. I spot Sarah at the register helping Mr. Jenkins, the janitor from my high school days. I steer Jake and Maggie toward the children's section, watching Sarah to see if she looks up. She doesn't.

Okay, so maybe I had an ulterior motive for coming here.

I thought Sarah and I were getting along pretty well the other day when I helped her with the shelves. She's the kind of woman I would've instantly noticed at some downtown bar somewhere: classy and polished, with that aloof, unattainable vibe. And yeah, I'll admit it was kind of fun to play the role of the country boy flirting with the cute city girl. She seemed to be into it, too. But when I asked if she wanted to hang out, she clammed up. I guess I can't blame her. She's new here, and I'm just a random "handyman" she got stuck with in a nearly empty building. Makes sense to be cautious.

But today, if she happens to see me with my niece and

nephew, and then happens to realize that I can be trusted to spend an evening with...well, that's not the worst outcome, is it?

I'm browsing a nonfiction shelf near the kids' section when Sarah finishes with Mr. Jenkins, then heads toward Jake and Maggie.

"Hi there, can I help you guys find a book?" Sarah asks them. Her back is toward me, and my eyes do a quick down-up. Not enough to be creepy, but enough to let me know that she looks damn good in those jeans.

"I don't like books," Jake declares, and I internally groan. That's what I get for putting my dating prospects in the hands of a seven-year-old.

"All right," Sarah says, laughter in her voice. "What *do* you like, then?"

"Dragons."

She runs her finger along a row of books, then pulls one out and shows it to Jake. "*How To Train Your Dragon,*" she reads.

"I saw that movie!" Jake blurts.

"Well, the book is way better." Sarah hands it to him. He takes it with all the enthusiasm of a kid being ordered to eat his broccoli, but he does start flipping through the pages.

Then Sarah crouches down next to Maggie. "What about you? What do you like to read?"

In response, Maggie shrugs. I know Bianca would scold her for being impolite, but I hang back and watch it unfold.

"Let's see," Sarah says slowly, then pulls out a book with a purple cover. "Do you like...fairies?"

Maggie brightens and looks over at me. "Uncle Jonny, will you buy me one of these?"

Sarah pivots, freezing when she sees me. "Oh. Are these your..."

"Niece and nephew," I say, coming closer. "Thanks for helping them."

She's so pretty. The thought floats through my mind. She's wearing a striped black-and-white sweater under a red apron that reads THE BOOK NOOK, her dark hair cascading over her shoulders, her lips all pink and pouty.

Unfortunately, the expression on her face is somewhere between wary and suspicious.

"Happy to help," she says, straightening as she notices the bag I'm holding. "Have you been doing some shopping?"

"Needed more dilly beans." I roll my eyes. "My little sister's going through them like potato chips."

Sarah blinks. "Your little sister?"

"Yeah. It's her first pregnancy, and I guess this is what the baby wants—her husband travels a lot for work, so I'm her first call."

"Oh." Sarah blinks again, and that wary expression eases. Then I remember when Sarah got a little weird last time we talked, it was right after Kara called and asked me to grab her dilly beans. Sarah must've thought...*gross.* I internally shudder.

"How've sales been?" I ask, wanting a new topic. "Converting Azalea to the joys of literature, one reluctant reader at a time?"

She shakes her head, but she's smiling now, which seems like a win. "Not sure I'm actually converting anyone."

"Hey, miracles happen." I nod toward Jake. Against all odds, he now appears to be actually reading the dragon book. "Look at him—future bestselling author in the making."

She chuckles. "Or a future professional dragon-rider. Hard to tell."

"Exactly my point," I say, grinning. "Either way, your influence is undeniable. You've got magic powers, basically."

"Magic powers, huh?" She folds her arms, peering up at me. "And what are your powers, Uncle Jonny?"

I pretend to think, tapping my chin. "Oh, I don't know... charming smile? Ability to carry giant boxes without breaking a sweat? Being the best uncle in the universe?"

She rolls her eyes, laughing. "And so modest, too."

"What can I say? Greatness is a burden." I shrug. "How are you liking Azalea so far?"

"I haven't explored it a whole lot. Been busy setting all this up."

And that's my in.

Leaning closer, I say, "Then you deserve a break. Not sure if you heard, but the lighting of the town Christmas tree is tonight. Want to come?"

I figure if there's any scenario where she'd feel comfortable hanging out with me, this is it. Public place, wholesome setting.

"I don't know," she says. "I've been pretty tired at the end of the day."

"Sure, but you have to eat dinner, right? There'll be taco trucks, funnel cakes, chestnuts roasting on an open fire..."

I grin, raising my eyebrows, but she shrugs and looks down. "Maybe I'll see you there?"

Disappointment pings through me. She probably has a boyfriend back home. Or maybe she's just not into me. Either way, the message is clear: Sarah is immune to my charm. I wonder if she's heard anything; there's nothing this town likes more than spreading gossip. Even if it's more than a decade old.

"Sure," I say, straightening up. "Well, I hope you get some good sales—"

"WHAT THE HELL IS THIS?"

Jake's high-pitched voice echoes through the bookshop. I whirl around; he's wandered into the romance section and has pulled a book off the shelf. The cover has a shirtless man with an oiled-up chest kissing a woman.

I'm about to burst into laughter when I see who else overheard him: Nancy Barnes. My tenth-grade English teacher. And she is not amused.

"Jacob McKay," she says sternly, peering down at him through her bifocals. "You ought to put that book down right now."

"Excuse me," I say to Sarah, then jog over to Jake. I got on Mrs. Barnes's bad side plenty of times in high school, and while I definitely earned it, I'm not about to let my seven-year-old nephew get the brunt of it.

"And you know better than to use that kind of language," Mrs. Barnes is saying, her voice sharpening. "That is unacceptable, young man—"

"Uncle Jonny says if it's in the Bible, we can say it," Jake cuts in, eyes flashing with defiance.

At that, Mrs. Barnes turns and sees me. She shakes her head, lips pressed together. "I should've known. Jonny McKay, back in town, already corrupting the youth."

I suppress an eye roll. Not that I blame her—I was a total shit in her class, when I bothered to show up. I scratched curse words into my desk with a paperclip, tried to pass off my older siblings' papers as my own, and generally made her life miserable at every turn. But come on, it's been *fourteen years*. "Mrs. Barnes, please—"

But then I feel a hand on my arm and look down; it's Sarah. I didn't even know she'd followed me over.

"Hi there," she says to Mrs. Barnes. "Can I help you find anything?"

Sarah's voice is customer-service perfect, but there's a tremor of tension beneath it. She's as pissed as I am about Mrs. Barnes chewing out Jake.

Mrs. Barnes's sharp gaze zeroes in on Sarah's hand on my arm.

"You'd do well to keep your distance from this one," she says, her tone icy. "He's trouble. Always has been, always will be. Best thing he ever did for this town was leave."

My jaw clenches. It's too late to change what Mrs. Barnes thinks of me, and Sarah's already made it clear she's not interested. But Maggie and Jake are watching, absorbing it all.

I'm about to say something when Sarah's hand wraps around my biceps, pulling me a little closer. Surprised, I look down at her.

"The tree-lighting," she says, looking up at me. "What time does it start?"

CHAPTER 5

SHIRA

24 DAYS UNTIL I CAN LEAVE

I'm not sure what Jonny did to the over-fifty female population of this town, but they clearly haven't gotten over it. At least when the woman at the taqueria said Jonny was trouble, she said it with love in her voice. The woman today was just mean.

Sure, he's an aggressive flirt. And fine, he seems a little cocky. But Jonny's been nothing but kind and helpful to me since the day I met him. Which, granted, was less than a week ago. But still. I couldn't ignore the way she was talking to him.

And what's my reward for being such a mensch? A maybe-date with said troublemaker for the town's Christmas tree lighting. What even is my life?

According to my friends—who were thrilled to find out that Jonny is an uncle-to-be and not a dad-to-be—I've got to lean into my main character energy; to forget about any inhibitions and fling like I've never flinged before.

In other words, act less like myself and more like Talia. Unfortunately, I'm the one who packed my suitcase, and instead of my friend's low-cut, midriff showing wardrobe, I've got my own boring tops and light sweaters for the mild Texas winter.

The town square is buzzing with holiday cheer when I walk up. It seems like everyone in Azalea is here, jockeying for position and trying to get the best view of the tree. It's not Rockefeller Plaza big, but it's at least twenty or thirty feet high.

I should have let Jonny pick me up—Chicago dating rules be damned. There's no way I'm going to find him in this crowd, and I have no clue which of the tents is the one selling hot cocoa. Scanning the square, I notice (not for the first time) just how white this town is. And most of the men are wearing a Carhartt jacket like Jonny's. It's like a real-life Where's Waldo—which reminds me, I should get a few more copies in stock.

I'm seriously considering giving up and going back home when I spot him walking toward me, a little girl with blond pigtails bouncing on his shoulders.

So, it's not a date, then.

That's okay, I try to convince myself. Less pressure, no expectations. I can just have fun and pretend to be a girl who goes to Christmas tree lightings. Maybe one of the other Carhartt guys will be down to hook up.

"Well, hello there," Jonny says, grinning as he approaches. "If it isn't the prettiest bookseller in all of Azalea."

"The only bookseller," I say, even though the compliment makes me feel tingly, like there's champagne running through my veins.

"Say hi, Emma."

"Hi, Emma," the little girl repeats, cracking herself up.

"Remember what I said about that hot cocoa?" There's a playful warning in his voice.

"Hi, Uncle Jonny's pretty friend," she says.

"Much better," he says, then leads me toward the hot cocoa stand where we were supposed to meet.

I recognize one of the kids behind the table from the 4-H stall at the Christmas Market (which I had to look up because where I grew up, in the northern suburbs of Chicago, people paraded their Gucci bags around, not their livestock).

"Three hot cocoas," Jonny says, giving the young man a twenty. He waves away the change but does ask for a tray to carry them, which I take, so he doesn't drop his niece from her precarious perch.

"Everyone's excited to meet you," Jonny says as we walk around the square's perimeter, where people aren't packed in quite so tight.

"Who's everyone?" I ask, nerves making their appearance known again.

"Oh, just my family." He takes a sharp right through the crowd, where a small group of kids and adults are gathered around a park bench.

"I want my hot cocoa!" Emma shouts, drawing everyone's attention.

Jonny bends to let her off his shoulders, and when he stands again, he says, "Everyone, this is Sarah. Sarah, this is almost everyone!"

He explains that his dad and his sister are both on bed rest for different reasons, but I meet his mom, who is warm and welcoming. Then Jonny introduces me to his older sister Bianca, her husband, and their kids—Maggie, the one who loves fairies, plus twin toddler boys named Liam and Logan, squirming in the double stroller. Next up is Jonny's brother, Isaac, who looks like a sterner, older version of Jonny, and his wife, Annabel. Jake (the one who said "hell" at the bookshop) belongs to them, as do Emma and a chubby baby girl who's fast asleep in Isaac's arms. There are hugs and handshakes and too many voices talking at once, and I'm overwhelmed in the very best way.

I'm talking with Jonny's mom and Bianca about the book-shop when Jonny places a warm Styrofoam cup in my hand. He steps behind me, and his breath tickles my ear as he says, "I put a little Bailey's in ours."

Trouble indeed.

The ceremony starts about thirty minutes later, and I'm feeling all warm and cozy thanks to the spiked hot cocoa and the hospitality of Jonny's family. They really are lovely—all of them tall and sturdy and friendly, constantly teasing each other and laughing like something out of an old sitcom. As an only child of two only children, I've always been fascinated by big families.

The pastor of the town church (or is he a Preacher? A Reverend? A Priest?) welcomes everyone and thanks the sponsors, including the new and improved Christmas Market. Jonny's mom looks at him, beaming with pride.

My parents could learn a thing or two from Mrs. McKay—being so proud that her son is a handyman for one of the companies sponsoring this event. I can't remember the last time I felt that kind of support from my family; maybe when I won the school spelling bee in third grade? That was probably my last crowning academic achievement before I broke my parents' hearts, revealing myself to be more of a book nerd than a nerd-nerd who was (and still is) allergic to math.

"And now," the pastor/preacher/priest says, his voice booming, "it is my great honor to introduce our choir, the Azalea Angels. I hope you'll join us—sing like no one's listening and loud enough for the Lord Himself to hear."

The crowd cheers as the choir kicks things off with "Oh, Christmas Tree." I thought I knew the lyrics—it's impossible to grow up as a kid in America without having a passing knowledge of popular Christmas songs—but after we sing about the lovely branches, I'm lost.

Jonny, however, is singing loud enough that people in heaven must be reaching for their earplugs. What he lacks in talent, he makes up for in pure Christmas spirit. An older couple sitting on a nearby bench gives him the side eye, but his nieces and nephews are delighted. I am, too—especially since he's pulling attention away from me and my lack of lyrical knowledge.

Next, the choir starts "Deck the Halls." I'm not the only one who doesn't know all the verses, but I do my best to make up for it when it comes to the fa-la-la-la-las.

Jonny's enthusiasm is contagious; he throws his arm around my shoulder, and I lean into his side. For one glorious moment, it almost feels like I belong here: in the middle of a small Texas town with a big, loud family, kicking off the Christmas season with bowels of holly. *Wait—that can't be right?*

Oh, screw it. I tip my head back and join in another rousing round of fa-la-la-la-la.

Unfortunately, the spirit dissipates as soon as the choir starts in on the next song, "O Come, All Ye Faithful." Even though I do know a lot of the words, it feels disrespectful to sing about something I don't believe in.

I can feel Maggie watching me, looking confused about why I'm not singing.

"Bathroom," I tell Jonny. "Be right back."

"I'll walk with you," he says.

"No, it's okay. Stay here, I'll come back."

"Promise?" He holds his pinky finger out.

Grinning, I shake my head but wrap my finger around his. "Promise."

By the time I make it back, the choir is singing "White

Christmas." Finally, a song I know every single word to. I also happen to know it was written by Irving Berlin, a fellow member of the tribe.

It feels like a scene from a holiday movie—the only thing missing is actual snow, which is meteorologically impossible since the temperature doesn't seem to drop below the mid-forties. Yet as if on cue from a director waiting in the wings, a fluffy white substance starts falling from the sky.

It can't be.

I reach up to touch it and smile as the soapy mixture melts in my hand. The moment still feels infused with magic, and I glance behind me at Jonny, who's watching the scene unfold with the same amazement as his young nieces and nephews.

He sees me looking at him and flashes me that disarming smile of his, then reaches over to wipe soapy bubbles from my nose. We're facing each other, eyes locked, as the song ends and someone on stage starts the countdown.

10.

9.

8.

The butterflies in my belly flutter.

7.

6.

5.

My gaze drifts down to Jonny's lips.

4.

3.

2.

I take the tiniest step toward him...

1.

The Christmas tree lights up, and I startle, taking a giant step back. There are enough lights wrapped around the tree to make it feel like it's the middle of the afternoon.

The crowd erupts with applause and cheers, waking Jonny's littlest niece, who starts crying in her daddy's arms.

Soon, two of the other kids join in, a chorus of complaints about being tired and hungry. It's decided that the party is over, at least for the McKays.

I turn to say goodnight to Jonny and thank him for what ended up being a truly wonderful night when he says, "Can I walk you home?"

CHAPTER 6

JONNY

24 DAYS UNTIL CHRISTMAS

"Thank you for coming tonight," I say to Sarah as we head down the street. The sound of Christmas carols and the crowd fades, replaced by the rumble of an occasional car passing. "Made it a lot easier."

She seems surprised. "Easier?"

I shrug. "My family...they should come with a warning label: high-decibel levels, unwanted opinions, and frequent chaos."

"Yeah, they're a lot," Sarah says, smiling. "But not in a bad way."

I glance over at her. *So damn pretty.* Tonight, she's wearing a navy wool coat over an ivory sweater, her dark hair pulled half-up with a sparkly clip, and tiny earrings that catch the light when she moves. There's something so...put-together about her. Sophisticated but relaxed. Effortless.

"You held your own like a champ tonight," I say, then bump her shoulder lightly with mine. "Now c'mon, tell me about you."

"What do you want to know?"

"Everything."

She arches an eyebrow at me. "Everything? That could take a while."

"I've got time." I slow my walking speed dramatically. "We'll start with the basics: where you're from, what you do for fun, then we can move into your deepest, darkest secrets..."

She laughs, warm and easy, and it makes me smile. Then she tells me she's always lived within two hundred miles of Chicago. She left to go to college in Indiana but moved back home after graduation and started working for Conor.

"I love Chicago," I tell her. It's where I met Conor, though for some reason I don't feel like sharing that. Maybe because it's clear he's a dick boss, and I don't want her to think I'm like him. "I lived there for a couple of years."

"You did?" Her eyebrows lift.

"Ah, the look of utter shock that I'm not just a small-town hick."

She flushes. "Sorry, I didn't mean—"

"I know. I'm teasing you." I flash her a grin. "Chicago's a great city. Amazing food, friendly people, beautiful lake. Terrifying winters, though. Almost lost a toe to frostbite."

I shudder, and there's that laugh again. It's nice to see her loosening up a bit. Getting comfortable with me.

We turn onto Main Street as we chat about Chicago. Turns out we've got a few favorite spots in common including Saturday mornings at Green City Market and live music at Joe's on Weed. I manage to steer clear of why I lived there, though, and not just because of Conor. My older brother's voice is in my head: *We get it, Jonny, you went to fancy business school. No need to work it into every conversation.*

And while I doubt Sarah would respond like that, it still makes me think twice about bringing it up.

"So...that lady at my shop earlier said something about you

being *back*," she says, glancing over. "You haven't been living here recently?"

"Ah, Mrs. Barnes." I rub the back of my neck, heat creeping in at the reminder. "Yeah, I've lived in a bunch of places. Most recently, L.A."

Before that, Seattle, Denver, New York, Atlanta, Boston, even some time in London and Amsterdam. Other than Chicago for business school, I haven't stayed anywhere longer than a year since college. It's been eight years since I graduated from the University of Texas at Austin, and I've barely spent more than a couple of days at a time in Texas since then.

"What brought you back here?" she asks.

I could tell her the truth—that I sold a start-up and I'm sitting on more money than I know what to do with. I know I should feel accomplished. Instead, I feel like a boat that's slipped its anchor. Totally adrift.

But that's not the kind of thing you share when you're just starting to peel back the surface of someone.

"My family needed me, and I'm between jobs right now anyway," I say, keeping my tone breezy. No need to mention how it gnaws at me, the question of what to do next. How unsettled I've felt.

She tilts her head, studying me. There's curiosity in those big brown eyes of hers; I can tell she doesn't quite buy my brush-off.

"Are you planning to stay here long-term?" she asks.

"Nah." I flash a grin, determined to steer us back to safer ground. "I'm a rolling stone, baby. Can't pin me down."

Her laugh bursts out, bright and unguarded, and my chest loosens. This is better—Sarah smiling, leaning in, sparks catching between us instead of illuminating the stuff I'm not quite ready to face.

I guide the conversation around to her again—her job, her

goals, where she falls on the deep-dish pizza debate (she's Team Pequods, which I can respect). She talks with her hands, and it's cute, the way her gestures get bigger the more passionate she is about the topic. And it's clear that she's passionate about her group of friends. She tells me about the girls she met in college and all the things they do together— brunch on Sundays, wine on Wednesdays—but she doesn't mention any family.

"And you'll be staying here until Christmas?" I ask.

She nods, but her expression tightens, like I brushed against a bruise.

"Are you okay with being away from your family for the holidays?" I say, more carefully.

Another pause.

"My parents split up when I was sixteen," she says slowly. "Holidays aren't really a big family thing anymore. Not everyone has a whole mess of siblings and nieces and nephews like you, Jonny."

The teasing lilt in her voice doesn't quite cover the sadness beneath it. I want to ask more, but before I can, a pickup slows as it nears us.

"Be careful, girl!" a voice calls. "Jonny McKay's gonna hit it and quit it, like always."

It's Dusty Hermanson, one year below me in school, arm dangling out the open window.

"Move along, Dusty," I say, keeping my voice flat.

Instead, he pulls the truck to a stop, eyes a little glassy as he leers in Sarah's direction. "You really want to be another notch in his belt, sweetheart?"

She tenses, and I shift so she's behind me. "Dusty," I say, voice sharpening. "Get on home. Now."

His gaze shifts back to me. "Can't blame you, man. Girl's got a hell of an ass—"

"Shut your fucking mouth." My voice drops, and my fist clenches. "Bet you've got some open containers in there. Should I call the sheriff and let him know?"

That wipes the stupid grin off his face. Dusty mutters something under his breath and peels out, tires spitting gravel.

I roll my shoulders, adrenaline still buzzing through me. Turning back to Sarah, I see her watching me with wide eyes. "I'm sorry about that," I say, gentling my voice. "He's an idiot, still bitter that his high school girlfriend asked me to Sadie Hawkins."

And made out with me in front of him.

Her lips press together like she's trying not to show how shaken she is. I want to reach out, tuck her closer, prove she's safe with me. But after what Dusty just said, I don't want to overstep.

Then her hand finds mine. Soft, deliberate. Our fingers lace, and warmth creeps up my arm. My muscles loosen, and I catch a whiff of her scent, vanilla and something floral. We start walking again, slower now, like we're both trying to drag out this moment. Overhead, the moon peeks out from behind a cloud, and across the street, the diner door swings open, letting out a wave of laughter and Christmas music. For the first time since coming back to Azalea, I'm almost at peace.

Something about this girl makes me feel relaxed and excited at the same time. It's been a while since I've dated, too busy to put much time or effort into it. Maybe I'm just lonely, stuck in my tiny hometown, and it's nice to be around someone who isn't from here?

Especially a very pretty someone who smells good and laughs at my dumb jokes.

"What's your story, Jonny McKay?" she asks after a bit.

"My story?"

"I've now heard three people reference your bad reputation." She says it lightly, but I can hear the genuine concern beneath.

I hesitate, considering how much to get into. There's the shoplifting, the cheating in school, the underage drinking. I made my mom cry more times than I can count, got myself declared a public disgrace by my then-mayor dad. And of course, all those times I got caught in "compromising positions" with girls who were definitely *not* innocent bystanders—but somehow it became my fault.

Such a cliché. The rebellious kid from the upstanding family.

"It's all deserved," I say finally. "I was a pretty rotten teenager."

Her eyebrows raise. "But that's got to be, what, more than a decade ago?"

I nod, mouth twisting. "Small towns have long memories. Once you get a reputation, it's hard to shake. Part of why I don't spend a ton of time here." Before she can ask more, I say, "I'd like to hear about *you* as a teenager. Let me guess: good kid, straight A's, maybe student government?"

She blushes. "Yeah, actually. Student council president."

"Knew it," I say, grinning with satisfaction. "Tell me, Madam President, what was your big platform?"

Soon, we're laughing again as she describes her grand plans to revolutionize the school's cafeteria offerings, and how it all went wrong when the school board switched to a vegan vendor who put beans in everything, leaving everyone so gassy that the teachers signed a petition, forcing the board to switch back.

Before we know it, we're standing in the driveway of the Petersons' place. She's renting out their mother-in-law suite, a free-standing cottage back behind their house. Hopefully Mrs. Peterson hasn't mentioned anything to Sarah about the time during senior year when I brought her daughter Katie home two hours after curfew smelling like Jack Daniel's with a couple of new hickeys on her neck.

"This is me," Sarah says, stopping at the bottom of the porch steps.

We're still holding hands, and neither of us seems in a hurry to let go. I tug her a little closer, and her gaze lifts to meet mine. My pulse kicks up.

"I had a really nice time with you tonight," I say softly.

"Me, too."

"Want to do it again?" I raise my eyebrows. "Maybe without my circus of a family hanging around?"

She nods, smiling. "I'd like that."

The porch light spills across her face, highlighting the soft curve of her lips, the shadow of her lashes. Her eyes drift to my mouth, her lips parting slightly in an invitation that's impossible to ignore. I lean down—

A car rattles past, someone whistling out the window.

I pull back with a sigh. "Well, that's one way to kill the mood."

She gives a nervous laugh and tucks her hair behind her ear. "Um...do you want to come in for a bit?"

My gut reaction is *yes, hell yes,* but then Dusty's voice pops in my head: *He's gonna hit it and quit it.*

After all the shit Sarah's heard about me—and after I basically confirmed that it's true—I hate the idea of her thinking I invited her out tonight to get her into bed. Not that I'd mind getting her into bed. In fact, the thought is damn appealing. But for some reason, it feels important that Sarah doesn't believe that's all there is to me.

My mouth opens, shuts, then opens again. I search for the right words, but none come.

Her smile falters.

"Never mind." She steps back, dropping my hand. "It's late,

and I've got another busy day tomorrow, so...yeah. Have a good night, okay?"

Shit.

Before I can tell her I'd love to come in, she's disappearing behind her front door. And I'm left standing on the sidewalk like a dumbass who just fumbled the final moment of an otherwise perfect night.

CHAPTER 7
SHIRA
19 DAYS UNTIL I CAN LEAVE

I t's Saturday morning, almost a week after the Christmas tree lighting, and the market is bustling. I'm talking to Susan Landry, my first repeat customer, about a book she started and finished reading yesterday, when I spot a familiar six-year-old bounding into the shop.

I look up, expecting to see Uncle Jonny behind her, ready with another excuse to be "dropping by." But it's his sister, Bianca, pushing a double stroller.

"You don't read many stories that are character-driven but also packed with so much action," Mrs. Landry is saying to me.

"Absolutely," I agree, even though I haven't read the book, *Hello Beautiful*, yet. "It's wildly original."

Mrs. Landry tilts her head, looking at me curiously. "It's a modern take on Little Women."

I nod because I do recall hearing that about the book, then apologize and excuse myself to greet Bianca and Maggie. The little twin boys in the stroller—whose names I can't remember —are asleep.

"I've got a bone to pick with you!" Bianca says with a bright smile on her face.

I pause, hoping she's joking. Are all McKay's this confusing? Her brother shut me down the other night, making me feel like an idiot for inviting him in. But every day since, he's been dropping by, bringing me coffee or candy from the sweet shop, leaning across the counter with that crooked grin. But it starts and ends there.

Despite the girls' constant encouragement and Talia's long-distance coaching, my clever quips and innuendos aren't landing—he hasn't picked up on my attempts to do something outside the bookstore. Or he has, and he's not interested. I wouldn't be surprised if he's one of those guys who are all about the chase, and I'm not making him chase me very hard.

"That fairy book," Bianca says, running her hands through Maggie's ponytail. "I've read it at least three hundred times—I could recite it by heart. 'Once upon a time, there was a little pink fairy...'" she starts, proving her point.

"We need another book," Maggie says, and my heart swells.

"Maybe two or three," Bianca agrees, then nods at the sleeping twins. "And the boys are getting jealous of all our reading time—do you have anything about garbage trucks, by chance?"

I laugh. "I've got just the thing." I lead them toward the children's section where two other kids are sitting cross-legged on the new rug, surrounded by piles of books. Maggie joins them, picking a book to flip through.

Bianca looks proud and a little jealous. "I don't think I've read a book without pictures since I graduated from Azalea High."

"Well, if you want to change that..." I say, holding my hands out to the world of books she's literally standing in the middle of.

Bianca studies me, apprehensive.

"Tell me some things you like," I say.

"Hmm." She hesitates, then says, "I honestly don't know what I like anymore. I got married and started having kids, and it's like I'm not 'me' anymore, I'm 'Mom.' And don't get me wrong, I love my kids. I *love* them."

"But you want to hold on to the other parts of yourself, too?" I suggest, thinking of Anya, who dropped off our group chat after she had her daughter and moved to the suburbs two years ago.

We started the new group chat for logistics—Anya didn't need to be bothered with details of when and where the rest of us were getting together—but that became the place where we teased Talia about whoever she'd gone home with the night before, where Maya texted screenshots from the guys on the apps, and Naomi bemoaned the challenges of a long-distance relationship. Soon, the smaller group chat was the only group chat.

I feel a pang of panic at the thought of the girls texting each other on a thread without me. I may be out of sight, but I don't want to be out of mind.

"Exactly," Bianca says, bringing me back to the moment. She seems to relax, almost relieved I managed to pull this confession from her. "So do you have a book for that?"

"I do, actually." I walk the few steps toward the romance bookshelf—which, in hindsight, I maybe shouldn't have put right next to the children's section.

I skim the shelves until I find what I'm looking for.

"Start with this one," I say, handing her a copy of *The Idea of You* by Robinne Lee. It's the movie tie-in edition with Anne Hathaway and Nicholas Galitzine making out on the cover. I loved the book, but the ending made Maya so mad she swore off my book recommendations for almost a year. But I think Bianca will appreciate the fantasy of it all. And the spice.

"I think I saw this movie," Bianca says, turning it around to look at the back.

"The book is always better," I tell her. "Trust me."

"You know, I think I do." There's sincerity in her voice, like she's talking about more than this book. After a moment, she adds, "So...are you and my brother dating?"

If we'd been having this conversation over coffee, I would have spit my drink out.

"I'm...we're...no," I say, and then with more certainty, "we're not."

She blinks. "Really? Every time I've seen him this week, he's been talking about you. *Sarah says the bookshop's getting busier every day,* or *Sarah thinks the Main Street decorations look like something out of a Hallmark movie,* or *Sarah says the sweet shop's caramels are the best she's ever tasted.* I guess I just assumed..."

I cringe at the reminder that Jonny still thinks my name is Sarah. If he'd come inside after the tree lighting, I would have cleared that up. Not that it makes a difference since he isn't interested in me. Once I'm gone, it won't matter what my name is—and this version of me he's getting to know is more Sarah than Shira anyway.

"He's been dropping by every day," I say. "But that's it."

I've been friend-zoned before, but it stings a little more coming from Mr. Bad Reputation. It doesn't say a lot for me if the guy who collects notches on his belt isn't interested in getting my pants off. He's probably just bored, dropping by and flirting with me to kill time when he's not fixing stuff around the market.

Bianca frowns, studying me. "Huh. I really thought there was something going on at the tree lighting."

I shake my head, my cheeks warming. "Well, there definitely isn't. I thought there might be, but...he shut that down *fast.*"

The memory stings—how I was so caught up in the holiday magic that I forgot to be cautious, trusting Jonny enough to step out of my comfort zone and put myself out there. The second I asked him to come in, he just...froze like he was trying to figure out how to let me down easy.

When I texted the girls about it after, Talia was ready to catch a flight down here and punch him in the nuts. She thinks I should move on and find another guy to bang, but Maya and Naomi still have hope for Jonny. The only thing they all agreed on was that they're proud of me for putting myself out there. For all the good it did me.

Bianca narrows her eyes almost like she's studying me, and I have the strangest sense that she knows what happened, even if I'm not sharing everything.

"My brother's past is a little...colorful," Bianca says eventually, and I appreciate the softer description of what I already know were his rebellious years. "And I know he can come off like a cocky little flirt, but he's a good man. He's smart and loyal and kind—do *not* tell him I said that," she adds with a grin. Then she turns thoughtful again. "And I think he likes you. A lot."

"Maybe as a friend," I say.

Bianca looks solemn as she shakes her head. "As smart as my brother is, he can really be an idiot sometimes."

As if our conversation summoned him, Jonny walks into the store, full of swagger and a little surprise as he sees me talking to his sister. He's wearing his usual Carhartt, his tool belt slung around his waist. His hair looks like he just ran his hands through it, and I hate how good he looks.

"Am I hallucinating?" he says, throwing an arm around her shoulder. "What is my big sister doing in a bookstore? I didn't know you read anything longer than Instagram captions."

"Shush," she says, playfully swatting his arm. "Maggie and the boys needed a few books, and I'm getting one, too."

He looks impressed—and I'm impressed he doesn't make a cheap joke about what kind of book it clearly is.

"What are you doing here, anyway?" Bianca asks. "I thought you were on baby duty with Kara? Isn't Kyle in Austin today?"

"He is and I am," Jonny says. "Our dear sister wanted some kettle corn, and I thought Sarah might like some, too."

"How thoughtful," Bianca says, laying it on thick. "You must *really* like her."

Jonny gives us both a weird look. "Sure," he says. "And there's a flickering light over at the Quilted Corner that needs fixing."

"Your brother is the hardest working handyman in Texas," I tell Bianca, then say to Jonny, "They should give you a raise!"

Bianca laughs. "He does not need a raise—and he's not a handyman. Jonny, what lies have you been telling this poor girl?"

"I never lied," he says, looking me straight in the eyes. He lowers his gaze for a moment, then looks back up. "But I'm not a handyman."

"He's the mastermind behind this whole place," Bianca says, her voice filled with pride.

My jaw drops. "But you said..."

Jonny puts his hands in his back pockets, and it looks like he's bracing himself for me to be angry or yell at him. But he's right, he didn't lie—I made assumptions, which was equally wrong of me.

"Everything I've told you is true," Jonny says. "I'm between jobs and here to help my dad out with the holiday market."

"Between jobs," Bianca snorts.

Jonny shoots her a warning look. "B..."

But his sister just rolls her eyes at him, then faces me.

"Jonny started some fancy tech company and sold it for a whole bunch of money."

He shifts his weight. "All right now, that's enough."

"Don't downplay it," Bianca says, shaking her head at him. "How much did you sell it for? Ten million? Twenty?"

I stare at him.

"And he isn't just 'helping our dad out,'" Bianca continues, turning back to me. "Before this year, the holiday market was just a few local vendors in stalls down in an old barn. Jonny secured this space and reorganized everything. He brought you in, and a few other vendors from Dallas and Fort Worth. It's a totally different experience."

Jonny shrugs, clearly uncomfortable with his sister's praise.

"Wow," I say, replaying the last two weeks and all my interactions with Jonny, seeing them in a different light. And then— "Wait, so *you're* Conor's friend from business school?"

Jonny frowns, and I try to think of anything I've told Jonny that could get me in trouble at work. My stomach twists at the idea of Jonny and Conor talking, laughing about the way I practically threw myself at him. Oh, God, I'm such an idiot.

I can't wait to tell the girls about this new development— they'll either be thrilled (*he's a millionaire, babe!*) or pissed that Jonny is friends with Conor, an asshole by association.

"He wasn't my bestie or anything," Jonny says. "But he owed me a favor, and I called it in."

I nod, trying to take all this information in.

"Excuse me," a young teenage girl says. "Do y'all have *The Summer I Turned Pretty?*"

"We do," I tell her, grateful for the distraction. "Follow me."

When I return a few minutes later, Jonny and Bianca have their heads bent together, talking in low voices. Rather, Bianca's talking—or maybe lecturing—and he's listening with an occasional eye roll.

They pull apart as I approach, and I get the sense they were talking about me. What Bianca says next confirms it.

"Jonny, is there something else you want to say to Sarah?" she says in the perfect mom-voice that makes me think of Anya again.

"I was going to ask you this even if my nosy sister didn't butt in," he says, shooting Bianca a playful glare. "But there's a good cover band playing at The Dive Bar tonight, d'you want to come?"

Bianca clears her throat.

Jonny rolls his eyes in her direction, then looks at me. There's an intensity in his gaze that makes my stomach flip. "I'd really like to take you out tonight, Sarah. On a date."

CHAPTER 8

JONNY

19 DAYS UNTIL CHRISTMAS

The bar is packed when I open the door, a wave of warmth and music hitting us. Sarah glances back at me and hesitates, a nervous glint in her eyes.

I put my hand on her lower back and lean in. "Don't worry, it's just a small-town country bar."

She grips my sleeve. "Do not leave me."

"I'll be right by your side," I promise.

She takes a breath and nods, then heads inside. Her hair's in a sleek ponytail tonight, and my eyes drift down to the curve of her neck as I follow her. For a split second, I imagine leaning in and pressing my lips there.

Maybe later. If I'm lucky.

After the tree-lighting, I told myself that this wasn't a good time to get involved with Sarah or anyone else. I'm here in Azalea to help my family. So I spent the week focusing on just that: doing odd jobs for Mom, running errands for Kara, making sure the holiday market stays on track. And yet, every time I walked through that market, something pulled me toward the bookshop. Toward her. I couldn't help stopping by, chatting, teasing, and flirting a little. Still, it took Bianca to finally push me over the edge and ask Sarah out again.

Big sisters—bossy and annoying as hell. But I guess they've got their uses.

I haven't been to this bar in years, and the place is buzzing: the bartender pouring drinks, waitresses balancing trays, familiar faces everywhere. The walls are crowded with neon beer signs for Shiner Bock, Lone Star, Bud Light, and more. Christmas lights are strung around the stage, where the band is playing a country version of "Rockin' Around the Christmas Tree."

"What can I get you?" I ask Sarah as we make our way over to the bar.

The woman next to her orders a ranch water, and Sarah's eyes flick toward mine. "What's that?"

"It's a Texas classic," I tell her. "Refreshing, no frills, gets the job done."

"Can I try it?"

"Sure thing," I say, smiling. "Great choice."

I wave over the bartender—Russell Barrowes, my little sister Kara's age—and order a Corona with lime for me and a ranch water for Sarah.

When he comes back with our drinks, Sarah takes a sip of hers. "Mmm, this is good. Tasty."

We find a spot to sit as the band ends the song and everyone claps. I'm surprised by the wave of nostalgia I feel. People of all ages fill the room—some my parents' generation, others I recognize from high school, and younger ones who were probably in elementary school back when I lived here.

Sarah leans in, her eyes darting toward mine. "Hey, so, I didn't know you were, like, a millionaire. Or, I guess a...twenty-millionaire?"

I shake my head, heat crawling up my neck. "Bianca's exaggerating." *A little.* Still, it's more than I ever expected to have to my name.

"What kind of start-up did you sell?" she asks, taking a sip of her drink.

"A buddy and I developed glasses that track the amount of sunlight you're exposed to and send the info to an app," I say, leaving it at that. Most people don't care about the nitty-gritty.

But Sarah leans in. "Ooh, interesting. Is it so people can avoid getting sunburns?"

"Partly," I say, smiling at her curiosity. "It does track UV, but it also helps make sure you're getting enough light, especially in the morning. Improves mood, sleep—stuff like that. We sold it to a bigger company that's adding the tech to their wearables."

"What are you going to do with the money? Retire and live on an island somewhere?"

I was a little worried she might act differently around me once she found out, but she seems the same. It's kind of a relief. "Nah, I'd be bored in a week. I want to do something useful with it. Make a difference, you know?"

She nods thoughtfully. "Like invest in something?"

"Maybe. I've headed a few different start-ups, and I love the early stages—getting things off the ground. The energy, the chaos, the uncertainty — it's exciting. Once things start settling down, though, I get a little bored."

"That tracks," she says, smiling.

I tilt my head. "What's that supposed to mean?"

She shrugs, playful. "Nothing bad. Just...you've got start-up energy. You don't strike me as the kind of guy who's into the long-term follow-through. And that's fine, everyone has different strengths."

Her words make me pause. She's not wrong—my interest in a project fades when the daily grind sets in. I've been lucky, having more hits than misses overall. But lately I've been feeling a little tired of the churn and burn, wondering what it might be like to focus on something less temporary.

Then again...maybe that's not me. Maybe I'm the kind of guy who's good at the launch—but not the long haul.

The band switches it up, leading into a cover of "The Boot Scootin' Boogie," and everyone cheers and runs out to the dance floor.

I turn to Sarah. "Do you know this one?"

She hesitates. "The song, but not the dance."

"It's easy to learn. I can show you?"

She downs the rest of her drink, then nods. "Sure."

I take her hand, and we head out to the dance floor. The crowd sways and shuffles, boots tapping against the sawdust-covered floor, and I guide her through the line dance. She picks up the moves quickly, and soon she's kicking up her heels, spinning out in a grapevine.

By the time the song ends, she's flushed and laughing.

"Okay, that was fun," she says.

Next up is "Feliz Navidad," and I raise my eyebrows at her.

"I...think I could use another drink," she says.

"Ranch water again?"

She nods. When I return, Sarah drinks this one even faster than the first. "This really is good," she says. "Like a light sparkling margarita."

"Well, it's not exactly light on the booze," I tease, glancing up as my brother Isaac and his wife weave through the crowd toward us. "Hey! Y'all ditched the kids for a night out?"

"Your mama basically begged us to let her keep them for a while," Annabel says, smiling. "Hey girl, how are you?"

Sarah beams. "I'm doing well. How are you?"

"Good! I've been hearing from a bunch of my friends that they're loving having a bookstore in town," my sister-in-law says.

"And Bianca says your recommendations are great," Isaac adds.

Sarah flushes, clearly pleased. "That's...so nice. I've never run a bookstore before, so I'm just winging it."

"Well, you're doing a great job," I say, nudging her with my shoulder.

Isaac and Annabel fade into the crowd as the band starts up a country swing version of "Jingle Bell Rock."

I incline my head toward the dance floor. "Ready to dance again?"

The next couple of hours melt away in a blur of music, drinks, and laughter. I lead Sarah through some basic swing moves. She stumbles over my feet a few times, and we both end up doubled over laughing. At some point, she's swept away by Harv Lundy, who's pushing ninety but still dances like a pro, twirling her so fast she squeals. Next, she's asked to dance by little TJ Mitchell (who's not so little anymore, probably twenty-two), then she's pulled into a circle of women by Annabel, dancing and singing along to a twangy cover of "Santa Baby."

I lean against a high-top, drink forgotten in my hand, and watch. Her ponytail is loose, her cheeks are flushed. And damn it, my chest is doing something weird—a warm, fizzy sensation that has nothing to do with alcohol.

Isaac comes up next to me, beer in hand. "Sarah seems great," he says.

I nod, unable to take my eyes off her. "She's...fun. And funny. And we have fun together—"

I pause, realizing I sound like an idiot.

Isaac grins knowingly. "Okay, well, don't fuck it up."

I glance at him. "Why do you say it like that?"

"Like what?"

"Like you *expect* me to fuck it up?" I can hear the defensive-ness creeping into my voice.

My brother shakes his head. "I didn't mean it like that. I just meant...she seems great. And you seem to like her."

My shoulders relax as my eyes drift over the crowd again, finding Sarah, her face glowing as she dances. "Yeah. Maybe."

The lead singer grabs the mic and says they're gonna slow it down. The first lazy notes of "Chestnuts Roasting on an Open Fire" float out, and before I can even think twice, I set my drink aside and head toward her.

"May I?" I say, holding out a hand.

She comes easily into my arms, folding against me. All at once, I'm aware of everything: her breath against my neck, the curve of her body pressed to mine. Damn it, I'm kicking myself for not asking her out sooner, for letting a whole week slip by when we could've been doing this.

"I'm sure glad Conor sent you here to run the bookshop," I murmur into her ear.

"Yeah?" she says, looking up at me.

I nod. "I thought he was sending a retired librarian, and it would've been kinda awkward to take her out tonight."

She giggles, swaying a little; she's tipsy, and it's cute. "I'm sure you would've charmed her anyway, Jonny McKay."

"Am I charming you?" I grin.

She shrugs, a mischievous glint in her brown eyes. "You're doing alright."

"Just alright? That's too bad. I'm aiming for an A+ grade."

"Well," she says, studying me. "You're surprisingly gentlemanly—"

"Surprisingly?" I raise an eyebrow.

"And even though you're an incorrigible flirt, you haven't flirted with anyone else in front of me yet—"

"I'd never—"

"—so I'd give you a...B so far."

"Brutal. You're a real tough grader, Ms..." I pause. "Wait, what's your last name?"

She hesitates. "Um. Schwartz."

"Ms. Schwartz," I say. "What can I do to bump that grade up? Any extra credit?"

"Let me think..." Slow and deliberate, her gaze drifts to my mouth.

My pulse kicks up. I lean in closer, so my lips brush her ear. "How many points could I get for a kiss?"

"Depends," she whispers.

"On?"

"On how good it is."

I smirk. "Oh, it's gonna be good—"

"Cocky."

"—but we're in public, so I can't go all out."

She pulls back enough to meet my eyes. "How about you give me a little taste, then?"

I swear the dance floor shrinks to just the two of us. Slowly, I lean down and brush my lips against hers. Her breath hitches, and I feel a tiny tremor move through her body. Even though I meant to leave it at that, I can't seem to help myself from going back in again. One brush becomes another, and when her lips part, I sink in deeper, letting the warmth pull me in. My hand slides to the small of her back, drawing her closer. God, her mouth is perfect. Luscious and soft and impossibly sweet, and when her tongue meets mine, it's like sparks ignite along my spine.

But there are way too many people around, so reluctantly, I pull away.

She's gazing up at me, eyes wide, a little dazed. "Not bad," she murmurs. "That'll raise you to a B+."

I shake my head, mock-disappointed. "How do I get that A+?"

She bites her bottom lip. "Maybe take me home and find out."

A few minutes later, we're out the door, hand in hand, walking toward Sarah's place. Luckily, it's not too far away.

"I had the *best* time," she says, throwing her arms out. "This town is so cute, and everyone has been so nice, and to think I was nervous to come here!"

"You were?" I ask, smiling. Tipsy Sarah is dangerously cute. "Why?"

"Oh, I just...I don't know."

She sways, and I grab her hand to steady her. "Watch out. You didn't go easy on those ranch waters tonight."

"Oooh, those were soooo good," she gushes. "What's in them?"

"Tequila," I say. "And some sparkling water and lime juice. But Russ is known for a heavy pour."

"Well, I don't feel drunk at all!" she declares, then promptly steps off the sidewalk.

I wrap my arm around her waist before she can stumble. "Yeah, you seem totally sober," I say, laughing.

By the time we reach the Petersons' place, Shira can barely stand straight. The second I open the door and help her inside, she goes up on tiptoe to kiss me.

"No more of that tonight," I tell her, leaning back. "You've had too much to drink."

She pouts, all big brown eyes and soft lips. "You had just as many drinks as I did."

I didn't, because it's my job to get her home safely, but I just smile. "Sorry to break it to you, darlin', but I can hold my liquor better than you can."

"Yeah, you're a lot bigger than me." Her hands run up and

down my arms, squeezing my biceps like she's inspecting them for science. "All muscly and stuff. Better take me to bed."

A laugh bursts out of me. My mom always said drunk words are sober thoughts, so I'm seeing this as a good sign. "How 'bout I tuck you in?"

I lead her into the bedroom, and she wobbles, giggling. She immediately starts unbuttoning her jeans, and I turn away just in time. Pretty sure she wouldn't be thrilled tomorrow if she found out I'd watched her undress, though God knows I'm dying to peek.

When I risk a glance back, she's pulled on a giant t-shirt that says BBYO. No idea what that means, but she looks damn cute in it. It falls about halfway down her thighs, giving me a clear view of her curvy legs and the single sock she's still got on.

Heat crawls under my skin, my imagination way too eager to fill in what I didn't let myself see as she changed. What she'd feel like pressed against me. How easy it would be to tug that shirt up and off—

Knock it off. I scrub a hand over my face. If I don't pull it together, I'm going to do something stupid.

I fold back the covers and motion for her to climb in.

She does, then grips my forearm. "Stay. Please?"

Suddenly, every cell in my body wants nothing more than to curl up next to her, let her rest her head on my shoulder. And then...who knows? Best-case scenario, she wakes up a few hours from now, sobered up, sees me there, and maybe the sparks from the dance floor turn into something more.

But worst-case scenario? She wakes up to find a man in her bed, and panics. I'd never forgive myself for scaring her like that.

I glance down at her. Her hair's a messy halo across the pillow, those dark lashes already drooping. My heart thumps. I really, really don't want to leave.

But unfortunately, responsible Jonny has to win out over reckless Jonny tonight.

"I don't think so," I say, reluctant.

She huffs like it's a terrible injustice. "You keep rejecting me! I mean, what am I supposed to think? My friends think maybe you have a secret wife somewhere. Or you're embarrassed because you have a teeny tiny dick."

I cough out a laugh. "Well, neither of those is true—"

"Your sister said you like me, but nooooo, I think you're just bored," she goes on. "You're bored, so you flirt with me, but then you don't do anything about it, and that's very misleading, Jonny McKay. All that start-up energy, and you can't seem to get this started."

There's genuine hurt under the babbling, and it hits me square in the chest. She doesn't get it—how much I do want to do something about it. Which is exactly why I can't stay.

I lean over the bed, lowering my voice. "All right, listen. You want me to sleep over when you haven't had approximately half a bottle of tequila, I won't say no. Deal?"

She lights up, grinning. "Deal. Dealio. Dilly beans. What are dilly beans, anyway? Can I have some?"

"You're gonna have one hell of a hangover tomorrow," I say, shaking my head.

"Yeah, you better stay and make me breakfast in the morning," she mumbles, snuggling into her pillow.

I chuckle. "Ah, so this is all just a ploy to trick me into making you my famous bacon, egg, and cheese breakfast tacos?"

Her eyes droop closed as she exhales. "I don't eat bacon."

"What about eggs?"

"I love eggs," she slurs, curling deeper into the covers. "I love eggs so much. I would really, *really* love to eat your eggs, Jonny McKay."

I bite back a smile. "Another time."

"Rude," she sighs. "Oh, wait...there's something I need to tell you. About me."

"Oh yeah? What's that?"

Her eyelids flutter, her lips parting. I wait, but then she exhales and relaxes, drifting off. So I head into the kitchen, fill a glass of water, and return to place it on her nightstand.

For a second, I stand there, watching her sleep, and that weird fizzy feeling settles in my chest again. Dusty's stupid comment from the other night echoes in my mind, that I'm going to "hit it and quit it." At first, I was worried that Sarah would believe him and wouldn't be interested. Now a different thought sneaks in: What if that's what she *wants* from me?

It stings. I'll admit it.

So I smooth the hair back from her forehead, press the lightest kiss there, and leave before I can change my mind about staying.

As I drive home, my mind keeps circling back to Sarah's comment about my "start-up energy." That's how I've been for a long time—jumping into new projects, building them fast, then moving on. It's how I've done relationships, too: all fun and flirtation, no follow-through.

But then I remember that kiss at the bar. The anticipation of leaning in, the reluctance of pulling away. That feeling of wanting more and knowing I'll have to wait until we're alone to get it. Makes me wonder what it would be like to slow this all down, to stretch out each moment, to take my time for once.

That kind of thing hasn't interested me before. I've never been good at being patient, but something about her makes me want to give it a try.

CHAPTER 9

SHIRA

13 DAYS UNTIL I CAN LEAVE

I've missed my friends every day I've been in Azalea, but tonight is the first night I've missed one of our treasured traditions. It started during our first year at Indiana University: Maya and I were roommates, and we met Talia, Naomi, and Anya at one of the monthly Shabbat dinners the Hillel on campus hosted.

Our friendship was forged on those Friday nights, and we've managed to keep the tradition going even after we graduated and all moved to Chicago. Once a month on a Friday night, the five of us—four since Anya got married, and now three since I got sent to Texas—meet at someone's apartment for a home-cooked (or home-delivered) meal. We light the candles, we eat, we gossip, and we drink a bottle of wine or three. It's one of my favorite nights each month.

And tonight, I'm missing it. At least in person.

"Please tell me why you haven't boned this guy yet," Talia is saying. We're FaceTiming while we both cook in our separate kitchens, almost a thousand miles apart.

"We've kissed," I say in my defense.

"Over a week ago," Naomi chimes in. "If you were lesbians, he would have moved in already."

Talia nods solemnly in agreement. "Seriously, girl—what have you been doing?"

"A lot of things," I say. "He still comes by the bookstore every day, and we drove into Fort Worth to go ice skating on Tuesday night—my butt is bruised from falling so much—then we went out for dinner and ice cream on Wednesday, and last night we volunteered as Santa's Helpers, wrapping gifts that were donated for families in need."

"That's cute," Naomi says, but Talia does not look impressed.

"Holy shit," Maya says, stepping into the frame. "I know what's going on—it's obvious. You guys are dating!"

"YES!" Talia shouts. "That's it, that's your problem, Shir! You don't date a fling, you fuck them!"

"Easier said than done," I say. My memory from the bar last Friday is still a little fuzzy thanks to all those ranch waters, but I have an unfortunately clear memory of Jonny standing in my bedroom, looking at me before walking away. That makes two separate occasions where I put myself out there only to be shut down. I'm clearly not very good at being this other person, whoever she's supposed to be.

"Babe," Talia says. "It doesn't have to be that complicated. You're hot, he's hot. You're horny, he's a man..."

"Maybe he likes you too much to sleep with you," Maya suggests.

"Men are so weird," Naomi says, shaking her head.

"I'm serious," Maya says. "You've heard of the box theory. He's putting you in the relationship box."

"Now you've just got to get yourself back into the hook-up box," Talia says. "No more date nights out—invite him over to your place."

"He's coming over tonight," I tell them.

"Atta girl!" Talia says.

"Did you invite him over for Shabbat?" Maya asks. Her voice is softer now; she knows how hard the last few weeks have been for me. That as much as I love how jolly and Christmassy everyone and everything is, it's been hard knowing that I'm a square peg who doesn't fit into this town's round hole.

"Well," I say, drawing out the word. "Kind of. I made a brisket and challah—but he doesn't know it's for Shabbat. I haven't actually told him I'm Jewish."

Or my real name. I don't mention that to girls, though—I'm a little embarrassed at how long this has gone on. But I'm going to tell him tonight. No matter what.

Talia laughs. "I'm sorry—I just can't remember the last time I had to tell anyone I was Jewish."

"Come to Texas," I tell her. "The state isn't just red; this month, it's red and green. And I haven't been avoiding it; it hasn't come up."

It's mostly true. I mean, I could've brought it up any of the many times we talked about Christmas, or when he asked about my family or my friends. But I've been trying to blend in here, to keep my head down and make it through the month. Does a hook-up even need to know that much information about me? Plus, it feels tied to my real name, which he also doesn't know.

"He'll find out when he takes your top off later," Talia laughs. "Is that a Star of David around your neck, or are you just happy to see me?"

"That doesn't even make sense," Naomi says, rolling her eyes.

"Thank you, Naomi—at least I can count on one of you to have my back."

"Oh, don't get me wrong," Naomi says. "I agree with the

what, just not the how. If this guy likes you, he'll like all of you. Let him get to know you and see who you are. Your whole self."

"Your whole naked self," Talia says, raising a glass of wine toward the camera.

I sigh and shake my head, torn between the instinct to protect myself and the desire to be brave, to let Jonny see the real me. But more than anything, I hope that tonight, we can get back to where we left things on the dance floor last weekend.

An hour later, my little cottage smells good enough to eat. It takes me back to all the Friday nights I spent over at Bubbe's house—except I decided not to make her recipe. As nostalgic as her brisket makes me, I'm on a mission to impress this man, and Anya's brisket is the best I've ever tasted.

I texted her yesterday to get the recipe—apparently, her secret is real onions, coconut aminos, and ketchup. She knew I was gone for the month because she still follows me on Instagram, and she seemed happy to hear from me, although she didn't say anything about getting together when I'm back in town.

I'm checking on the potatoes for the seventeenth time when I hear Jonny's big blue truck coming down the long driveway. I give my hair a quick fluff and smooth out my top before walking to the door. At the last second, I slip my necklace out so the gold Star of David shines against the royal blue of my shirt.

It's a small gesture, but it feels good to be taking a little step toward reclaiming myself. When I first used my "Starbucks" name, I never imagined I'd be getting to know these people, that I'd want them to get to know me.

I open the door before Jonny can knock, and whatever anxiety or pressure I was feeling dissipates at the sight of him.

He's wearing the red flannel shirt he had on the night we met—the one that looked so soft I wanted to rub my face against the fabric. Only now, I can.

His face lights up when he sees me, and even though he's got a bottle of wine in one hand and a foil-covered dish in the other, I step toward him and give him a half hug, pressing my cheek against his sturdy chest. He smells like fresh air and spearmint, and the shirt is just as soft as I thought it would be.

"Well, hello there," he says, wrapping an arm around me to complete our quasi-hug.

"Hi," I say, stepping back. "Sorry about that."

"Nothing to be sorry about, I'll always take an opportunity to have a pretty girl's hands on me," he says, eyes twinkling as he hands me the bottle of wine. "This is from me, but the pie's from my mama."

"Thank you both," I say, closing the door behind him.

"What smells so good?" he asks, walking toward the kitchen. He seems to know his way around, and I remember he was here the other night, tucking me into bed like a little girl and getting me a glass of water to help curb my hangover since I apparently can't handle my alcohol.

A good reminder to stick to one glass of wine tonight, two at the most. I've got to strike the balance between liquid courage and staying in control so I can complete both of my missions tonight: tell Jonny my name and finally get his pants off.

"I hope you like brisket," I say.

"Like it?" Jonny says. "I'm from Texas. I love it!"

"Good—if you didn't, I was going to throw it in a tortilla and call it a taco." I slip on floral oven mitts that are decidedly not sexy, but neither are third-degree burns. And I have big plans for these hands later tonight.

"What can I do to help?" Jonny asks.

"Open the wine?" I point him toward the drawer with the corkscrew.

A few minutes later, we're sitting around the kitchen table, a Jewish feast before us: the aforementioned brisket, roasted potatoes seasoned with Lipton onion soup mix, green beans, and fresh challah.

"Whoa," Jonny says after his first bite. "This doesn't taste like any brisket I've ever had before."

"I hope that's not a bad thing?"

Jonny shakes his head emphatically. "Are you kidding? It's amazing." He takes another bite and groans in pleasure. The sound stirs something inside of me; I want to hear it again later and be the reason he makes it.

"It's a friend's recipe," I tell him. "How do you make it in Texas?"

"We smoke it. All of the seasonings give it a bark, like a crust on the outside." Jonny's face lights up. "Want to come and try it? My brother's smoking one this weekend, and my mom's been bugging me to bring you over for dinner. She doesn't think you're eating enough."

"What? Why?" I may be short, but no one would ever accuse me of looking like I missed a meal.

Jonny shrugs. "Feeding people is her love language, and she'd love it if you came. I would, too. Will you?"

"Okay," I say. The idea of spending another evening in the company of Jonny and his loud and boisterous family sounds perfect. "When?"

"Sunday. Around four-thirty."

My stomach sinks.

Sunday is the first night of Hanukkah. The girls and I always spend the first night together doing a white elephant gift exchange. This year, they sent me a package to open, and we're planning to FaceTime before they go to a Shamash Bash a local bar is hosting.

"This Sunday?" I ask, stalling. For some reason, I can't bring myself to explain this, to tell Jonny why it's important to me. My mind whirls, searching for some other excuse. I can't exactly tell him I'm busy or that I have other plans—Jonny knows he's the only person I hang out with in town.

The girls won't mind if I bail. If anything, they'd get mad at me if I turned Jonny down just to light candles and talk on the phone with them. They're the whole reason I've been testing out this new version of myself—flirty and spontaneous, and forward. Blissfully free of my usual overthinking ways. At least *mostly* free.

They'd be the first ones to assure me that I'll have seven other nights to light the candles, but only one night where I'm invited to join Jonny's wonderful family for Sunday dinner. Still, my stomach is doing a weird, twisty thing.

I push past the guilt and say, "I'd love to."

And I'm pretty sure I mean it.

After dinner, Jonny helps me with the dishes, and we continue our easy conversation. I tell him about the bookstore, how I'm getting more customers every day, and how I'm ordering more stock—not just replenishing what I have but adding new titles. He tells me about how hard it's been being back in his parents' house, how he's happy to help out, but his dad is ornery and frustrated that he can't be his usual strong self.

"Thanks for helping with the dishes," I say when the last plate has been washed and dried.

He leans against the counter, flipping the dish towel over his shoulder. "My pleasure. You cooked, so I should've done all the dishes while you sat there drinking wine and looking pretty. But I kind of liked having you close."

He's watching me, eyes soft but intent, his lips in that half-smirk that makes my stomach flutter. The kitchen feels smaller suddenly, the hum of the fridge loud in the silence. It feels like there's a question hanging in the air: what happens next?

I take a step closer to him as Talia's words echo in my mind: *It doesn't have to be that complicated. You're hot, he's hot. You're horny, he's a man...*

I try to push any lingering self-doubt out of my mind, lift up on my toes, and go for it.

Jonny doesn't hesitate, leaning down to meet me halfway. When his mouth captures mine, the sound I make is embarrassingly eager. But he smiles against my lips, and his hands slip to my lower back, drawing me closer.

The next kiss is slower, almost lazy, like he's got all the time in the world. It's decadent: the taste of red wine on his tongue, the sweep of his hand up my spine, the thrum of pleasure under my skin. He's so much taller than me, and my fingers twist in his shirt as I try to tug myself higher, closer.

Without breaking the kiss, he reaches down and scoops me up, setting me on the counter. My knees part, and he steps between them, his hands coming to my face. I expect things to speed up now, to tip over the edge, but he keeps that same deliberate, unhurried pace. His thumbs skim my cheekbones as his tongue searches my mouth, all his focus right here, on me. Like there's nothing else in the world he'd rather be doing than this.

Heat builds low in my stomach, coiling tighter with every drag of his lips. I hook my fingers through his belt loops and tug him closer, craving the solid press of him against me, but he doesn't budge. His body is so close, his hips between my thighs, but there's a maddening inch of space between us. When I scoot forward on the counter, desperate to close it, he shifts back.

It's the sweetest kind of torture. My pulse is racing, my breathing erratic, and I can tell he's feeling it, too. I slide my hands beneath his shirt, feeling the heat of his skin against my palms. He hesitates for a beat, then dives into another kiss, somehow even deeper. It's both infuriating and intoxicating, this sense that he's holding a match right above kindling and refusing to let it catch.

"You're going to make me fall apart," he murmurs.

"That's kind of the idea."

He huffs out a quiet laugh, pressing his forehead to mine. "If you only knew what I want to do to you."

Electricity sparks down my spine. "You could show me."

But he just exhales, a slow, shuddering breath that brushes against my lips. So I take his face in my hands and kiss him, my fingers sliding up into his hair. The second my nails graze his scalp, a low sound escapes him, half sigh, half groan.

"So good," he breathes. "That feels so good, Sarah."

I freeze. "Shira," I whisper, not sure why I chose *this* moment for my confession. Maybe because I want him to be moaning *my* name, to be feeling these feelings for me, not the person I've been pretending to be.

He's moved to the other side of my neck, but stops when he realizes I've gone rigid. He pulls back, looking at me with a concerned expression. "You okay?"

"It's Shira," I tell him, my voice a little wobbly. "Sarah is my Starbucks name."

"Your what?" Now it's Jonny's turn to stiffen. He steps back, eyes narrowing like he's seeing me for the first time.

"The name I give people when it doesn't matter—kind of like a nickname."

"But it's not your name?"

I shake my head, my cheeks warming under his sharp gaze. "My real name is Shira."

"Shira," he repeats, like my name is a mystery, something strange and different. He shakes his head. "Okay, but—why would you tell *me* the wrong name?"

My stomach tenses, all the warm, lovely feelings turning to stone. I bring my hand to my necklace, rubbing my fingers against the sharp edges of the six-pointed star, knowing I have to fully rip the Band-Aid off.

"I'm sorry. It's just...not a common name, and it felt easier at first, when I didn't know I'd even see you again. I—I've been wanting to tell you that, and also—"

Jonny's phone rings, and we both flinch. He reaches into his pocket to silence it, but it immediately starts ringing again.

"Sorry," he says, fishing it out of his pocket.

I slip off the counter, drowning in embarrassment. I wish I could fast-forward past this part, or rewind to a few minutes ago when we were kissing like we were the only two people on the planet, or even further back to two weeks ago when he introduced himself and I told him my name was Sarah.

Why did I tell him my name was Sarah?

"Shit," Jonny is saying into the phone. "I'll be right there. Five minutes, okay? Take some deep breaths. Everything's gonna be all right. See you soon."

He hangs up and looks at me, and for the first time since I've met him, he seems genuinely worried.

"Is it your sister?"

He nods, moving out of the kitchen. "She's having contractions, and Kyle is at some sales conference in Austin. I have to go."

"You have to go," I agree, following him to the door

He grabs his jacket, then turns back to me, his head tilting as he studies me for a second. "Shira," he says, then shakes his head like he still isn't sure what to make of it. "Well, thanks for telling me."

"Thanks for not hating me?" I say, biting my bottom lip. "You don't hate me, right?"

"No," he says, but he seems distracted. And the quick kiss he places on my cheek feels platonic.

He's worried about his sister, I tell myself. Understandably so.

"There's more I want to tell you," I say, hoping I'll be able to explain and tell him everything else I've been less than honest about. Give him a chance to see the real me, including the pieces I've been afraid to show.

"We'll talk later," he says, then gives me another platonic kiss.

"Keep me posted on Kara," I say, and he nods before walking out the door. Leaving me alone and lonely and feeling like the jerk I am.

CHAPTER 10

JONNY

11 DAYS UNTIL CHRISTMAS

It's Sunday dinner at the McKay house, and Sarah isn't here.
I mean, *Shira*. Who I've hardly seen since rushing out of
her place on Friday evening.

Kara ended up being fine, but the doctors kept her
overnight for observation. She was pretty scared, though, so I
stayed awake with her until Kyle arrived in the morning. Even
though I hadn't slept, I felt bad about how I'd left things with
Shira, so I stopped by the bookshop to bring her an apple cider
donut from the bakery at the market.

Everything between us seemed fine then, and I went home
and slept until mid-afternoon. As soon as I woke up, Dad had
me fixing a stretch of fence he could see through the window.
He barked out orders from his recliner, while I worked outside
in the cold, cursing under my breath.

When I finally had a chance to recheck my phone, I saw a
text from Shira saying she couldn't make it to Sunday dinner
because she's not feeling well.

Now here I am, sitting in the dining room with the whole
family, wondering what happened. Everyone's laughing and

talking over each other, the table is crowded with smoked brisket, potatoes, and enough side dishes to feed the neighbors if they happen to drop by. I moved Dad's recliner so he can sit in his usual spot at the head of the table, and even Kara's here, released from her bed rest for a couple of hours as long as she doesn't lift more than her fork. The little kids are wiggling in their chairs, and the dogs are under the table, begging for scraps.

It's the kind of noisy chaos I grew up with, but my mind keeps drifting to Shira. I can't stop the little nagging worry in the back of my mind that I screwed up somehow. Maybe it was my brilliant idea to "slow things down" that turned her off. If she's just after a hookup, the invitation to family dinner probably didn't help. Or was it the way I reacted to the whole thing about her name? Or—

"Earth to Jonny," Dad booms.

I snap to attention. "Huh?"

"Bianca was saying the new Christmas Market has been a huge hit," Mom says, patting Dad's arm like she's reminding him to use his inside voice.

"Yeah," I say, forcing a smile. "It's great."

"I do have to point out one thing," Isaac says, dishing himself up another serving of potatoes. "Mom said you invited that bookseller, but I don't see her here. Guess all those college degrees can't help you get a date?"

I roll my eyes. "She was going to come, but she isn't feeling well."

"That's too bad," Mom says, frowning.

"Does she got a cold?" Maggie chimes in.

"Is she frowing up?" Emma adds.

"I don't think so." I'm taking another bite of brisket when I notice my sisters exchanging one of their looks. "What?" I demand.

Kara shakes her head. "You really are duller than a drawer full of spoons."

I bite back the urge to point out that I've built and sold multiple companies. None of that counts when your siblings still remember you peeing your pants during a thunderstorm in third grade.

"Yeah," Bianca says. "If a woman says she doesn't feel well, there's usually something else going on."

I set down my fork. "Like what?"

"Like you did something stupid?" Isaac suggests.

"Such as... calling her the wrong name for days?" Bianca suggests, and everyone at the table snickers.

Kara grins. "His brain's too full of knowledge to bother with little details such as a person's name."

I press my lips together. That was how I decided to explain the Shira-Sarah thing to my family: that I initially misheard her name. And of course, now they'll never let me live it down.

"She's been working long days at the bookshop," I say. "She's probably tired."

"No, you did something wrong. More than just the name thing." Isaac points his fork around the table like he's conducting a survey. "Ladies, am I right, or am I right?"

"He's not right," I say, but it's useless—Kara and Bianca are nodding in unison, Annabel's hiding a grin, and Mom has the same expression she gets when the dogs track muddy paw prints on her clean floor. Meanwhile, my brothers-in-law, Kyle and Chad, are giving me sad smiles of solidarity, which...doesn't help.

"Oh, Jonathan," Mom sighs. "What did you do?"

"Nothing!" My voice cracks like I'm fifteen again, and then the whole table erupts. Kara's saying I probably put my big dumb foot in my big dumb mouth, Bianca's claiming that most of a woman's problems come down to something a man said or did. Isaac's laughing around a mouthful of potatoes, and his wife is giving him an earful for riling everyone up. The baby's fussing, the twins start fighting over the last roll, and Kyle and Chad just sit there shaking their heads like they're tired of this circus. Voices pile on top of each other, louder and louder, until—

"That's enough!" Dad bellows, and everyone goes silent. He points his butter knife straight at me. "Whatever you did... fix it."

"For the last time, I didn't do anything," I say, even though a voice in my head says, *Did I?*

"Well, go figure it out," Dad says. "The rest of us would like to enjoy our meal without having to look at that expression on your face."

I scoff. "What expression?"

"Like you're some kind of slack-jawed moron."

Isaac snorts, then turns it into a cough when Annabel elbows him.

"And take that girl a plate of food," Mom adds. "I worry about her getting enough to eat, living all by herself. I bet Donna Peterson never feeds her."

"Fine." I shove back my chair, shaking my head. "Happy now, all you meddling McKays?"

My sisters nod, identical smug grins on their faces.

"Yeah, I'm happy," Dad says, picking up his fork. "Happy you're gonna do something purposeful instead of sitting on your ass."

"Language, Dad," Bianca scolds.

"It's in the Bible!" Dad bellows, triumphant. "Look it up!"

A few minutes later, I'm parking Dad's truck in front of the Petersons' house. My mind is bouncing between *what the hell am I doing* and *what if she doesn't want to see me* and *if I somehow hurt her feelings, I'm going to punch myself in the face.*

I grab the foil-covered plate from the passenger seat and climb out of the truck. I'm halfway down the driveway when I freeze.

The window to Shira's place is lit up, the curtains open. I can see her through the window, walking around holding her phone up like she's FaceTiming with someone. She's smiling. Laughing.

Definitely not sick.

But now *I'm* not feeling great. Clearly, she had something better to do tonight, even though it's just over the phone. What if it's some guy back home she's talking to? Some fucking dickhead guy making her smile and laugh like that?

My stomach clenches in a way I don't want to examine too closely. She ends the call after a bit, pocketing her phone and turning away. When she comes back over to the window, she's carrying something and sets it on the windowsill.

A menorah.

And then it all crashes down on me: what a complete and utter dumbass I truly am.

I'm frozen, watching as she strikes a match. Her lips start to move. She lights the center candle, then touches it to the first one. Her face glows in the candlelight, peaceful and soft, and for a minute, I just stare at her, transfixed. She really is so damn pretty.

But then...a tear trickles down her cheek. Her shoulders fold in on themselves. She buries her face in her hands—and starts sobbing.

The sight hits me like a punch to the throat. This is so much worse than when I thought she was talking and laughing with some guy. I should go to her. I should *do* something. But before I can, she disappears from the window. A few seconds later, the light turns off, leaving only the two glowing candles.

I stand there in the dark, clutching this stupid foil-covered plate, feeling split right down the middle. Part of me wants to run up those steps and knock until she lets me in. The other part—louder, meaner—is telling me I'll just screw things up more.

So I get back in the truck and drive home, my mind a whirling mess.

Why didn't she tell me? Or, no—better question: Why didn't I put the pieces together myself? My brain is sifting through our interactions over the past couple of weeks. Her name is Shira Schwartz. She didn't sing any of the religious songs at the tree lighting. *She doesn't eat fucking bacon.*

When I stop at a red light, I grab my phone and google BBYO, from that T-shirt she wore. Turns out, it's a Jewish youth group. Which, of course, it is.

Groaning, I lean my head back on the headrest. I am *so fucking stupid.*

But that's not even the worst part. The worst part is realizing I'm not someone she trusted enough to share this with. That she'd rather sit in her rented cottage alone, lighting candles and crying, than open up to me.

I know she was nervous to come here, but I thought she was relaxing around me. Letting me get to know her. Apparently not.

It's like having the rug yanked out from under me—only I'm also the one responsible for the yanking. I should've made her feel comfortable. I should've paid attention. I don't know what it's like to be Jewish, but I do know what it's like to feel out of place in this town.

I should've been the guy she could lean on. Instead, I'm just another clueless idiot she thinks she has to hide herself from.

. . .

I drive around for a while, until I've calmed down enough to think this through.

If there's one thing I've learned from growing start-ups, it's that you can't control everything that happens, but you can control how you respond. Doesn't matter if a vendor flakes, an investor bails, or the market takes a nosedive—my job is to take responsibility, adapt, and move forward.

That's the deal here, too. I can't force Shira to trust me. But if she doesn't feel comfortable being herself around me, then I sure as hell can take a hard look at why.

And I can do better.

By the time I get home, I've got a plan cooking in my brain. The house is quiet and dark, and my mom's in the kitchen, wiping down the counters.

The dogs greet me at the door, and I absently pat them. "Where's Dad?"

Mom glances at me, brow furrowing. "Watching the game. Is Shira okay?"

"Not exactly."

"Is it your fault?"

My jaw clenches. "Pretty much."

Before she can ask more, I head into the den and slump into the recliner next to my dad's.

"Well?" he says, eyes on the TV.

"I'm a slack-jawed moron," I say, sighing.

He nods, once. "Figured."

"Can you help me fix it?"

At that, he mutes the volume and faces me, his expression softening. "What d'you have in mind?"

I fill him in on my plan, and as I talk, a slow smile creeps over his face. "You must really like this girl," he says when I finish.

"I..." Swallowing, I remember that gut-squeeze when I saw her laughing on the phone, then the sucker punch when she started crying. "I just don't think anyone should feel that alone on a holiday," I say, finally.

"Uh-huh." Dad studies me, eyes narrowed. Then he clears his throat and leans back in his chair. "Now listen, you'll have to take the lead on this. Your mama'll have my guts for garters if she catches me in the shop."

"I'll do all the work. I just need some direction."

He hums, stroking his beard with one hand. "How big do you want it?"

"As big as we can make it."

His eyes twinkle. "You know what your Granddad McKay used to say—the bigger the screw up, the bigger the apology."

"Think we could put it in the town square?" I ask. "The opposite end from the Christmas tree."

"I'll talk to the city council—they'll approve it," Dad says. "We can have it ready by Tuesday night. Maybe Wednesday."

"You're gonna need food," Mom says from the doorway, where she's clearly been listening in. "Can't do something like this without food."

I nod, slowly. "That'd be great, but I don't know—"

"I'll take care of it," she says, turning and walking away.

I glance back at my dad, who rubs his hands together, grinning. "Guess we're about to make history in this town. Let's get started."

CHAPTER 11

SHIRA

8 DAYS UNTIL I CAN LEAVE

It's Wednesday, and I haven't seen Jonny since he dropped by the store on Saturday to bring me a donut and let me know his sister was okay.

I'd been so relieved that all seemed to be forgiven with the whole name thing—but now I'm worried that I screwed things up even more by bailing on Sunday dinner with his family.

When I texted on Saturday afternoon to tell him I wasn't feeling well, it wasn't an outright lie. The guilt of being "Sarah" the last two weeks finally caught up to me, and the thought of skipping the first night of Hanukkah made me feel like I was abandoning an important part of myself.

And I figured it would be better for Jonny and me to see each other again when it could be just the two of us, so that we could talk, and I could tell him everything I didn't get to before we got interrupted.

But I haven't seen him since, and it's making me worried. I could be reading too much into it; he did text me on Monday morning to see how I was feeling and let me know that he would be busy for the next few days, working on an important project with his dad.

He's been true to his word, and other than the occasional text, Jonny's been radio silent. I keep reminding myself that his dad is the reason he's down here in the first place, the reason that *I'm* even here. But I miss him, which I haven't admitted to the girls, since that's clearly not fling behavior.

Every time I catch someone out of the corner of my eye wearing a tan Carhartt jacket—which happens at least ten times a day around here—my pulse spikes, hoping it'll be Jonny sauntering in with a smile or a treat.

Of course, it hasn't been him. Not once.

Which is why, when the bell on the front door rings and I look over to see a tall, sturdy man with dark blond hair and a killer smile, wearing a Carhartt jacket, it takes me a second to realize it's actually Jonny.

"Hi!" I say, rushing toward him. I pause, not sure if I should hug him, kiss him, or shake his hand.

Luckily, he decides for me, leaning in to give me a quick hug and a kiss on the cheek. "You're looking really good," he says, his eyes slipping down my body in a way that makes me flush.

"This is what I always wear to work," I say, glancing down at my outfit—jeans, a sweater, and the branded apron, which has pretty much been my uniform down here.

"Like I said, looking really good." He grins. "You feeling better?"

"Much better." I cough, a phantom remnant of whatever illness I supposedly came down with.

"In that case, do you have any plans after work tonight?" Jonny asks.

I shake my head; he really is the only person I hang out with in this town, although a few of the older ladies have invited me to play dominoes with them.

"Good, then I'll pick you up here at six-fifteen."

"Okay," I say, trying to play it cool, and not like I'm bursting with excitement and relief. "Where are we going?" It's still Hanukkah, but I can always light the candles when I get home, before I go to bed.

"If I tell you, it'll ruin the surprise."

"A surprise?"

Jonny nods, rocking back on his heels, his mouth curved in a suspicious grin.

"Can I get a hint?"

"Nope," he says, a smug look on his face. "Just be here and ready at six-fifteen."

And with that, he's gone, leaving me with six and a half hours to try and pass without driving myself crazy with curiosity. Which is a hell of a lot better than driving myself crazy with regret like I have been. I already feel lighter, knowing Jonny doesn't hate me. Which is good, because I'm really starting to like him. A lot.

The rest of the afternoon crawls by like I knew it would, and during the long stretches without customers, I consider all the different surprises Jonny might have in store. I could see him planning something extravagant, like a helicopter ride around Azalea and neighboring towns to look at all the Christmas lights—he is a gazillionaire—or something small and low-key, like watching a drive-in movie.

Honestly, I'll be thrilled with whatever he's planned. It really is the thought that counts—just the fact that he planned something, that he missed me, too, means the world.

Around five o'clock, I'm about to crawl out of my skin when the bell on the front door announces another customer.

I look up to see an older Latino man with dark brown hair and tan skin, weathered by years of working in the sun. He looks like he's lived a lot of stories.

"Hi, there," I say. "How can I help you? Looking for yourself or for a gift?"

The man shuffles awkwardly on his feet, looking overwhelmed, like he's not quite sure where to start.

"Do you have books for niños...children?" he asks in a thick accent. "With English and Spanish?"

"I do," I say, leading him back to the children's section.

Once I realized how many bilingual families lived in this town, I placed a new order for Spanish-language books and several children's books that feature both languages.

"Right here," I say, pointing him toward the right spot on the shelf.

He's the only customer here, and I could use the distraction, so I stick around to help him pick out a few books. He tells me his name is Miguel and that he was born in Mexico, but he and his wife have lived in Azaela for more than forty years. Like so many of the people I've met over the last few weeks, he's grateful that the town finally has a bookstore, which makes me proud of this job in a way I've never felt before.

"You're going to be a very popular grandpa," I tell him, as I wrap the books he purchased.

He smiles like I'm the one who gave him a gift as he hands over the cash. The whole exchange leaves me feeling light, happy, and ready for whatever Jonny has up his sleeve.

As promised, Jonny is waiting for me outside the market at six-fifteen on the dot in the big, blue truck—his dad's, I now know. As soon as he sees me, he gets out and opens my door, offering his hand to help me climb in.

Definitely not something the guys I usually date ever do, but I could get used to it.

"Where are you taking me?" I ask once he's settled in the driver's seat.

Jonny laughs and shakes his head. "Didn't anyone ever tell you that patience is a virtue?"

I shrug. "I must have missed that day at school."

"Well, it's never too late to learn," he says, pulling out of the parking lot.

"You are torturing me, Jonny McKay."

He flashes me a smile and reaches his hand over, giving my thigh a little squeeze. His touch sends a shiver through me. All this flirting and build-up with no release is starting to get to me.

"So how was your day?" he asks. "Change anyone's life with a book?"

"I sold some children's books to a very cute grandpa," I say, thinking of Miguel. "And you know how Susan Landry's always coming in to chat about what she's reading? She was back again today. I can barely keep up with her."

"Did you get some good talking points from Goodreads about the book she read?" he teases.

"Believe it or not, I actually read this one!" I don't add that I read it in an attempt to keep my mind off him, and if he'd ever talk to me again.

"Oh yeah?"

"Yeah, *The Correspondent*. It's told in letters written to and from the main character—such a cool structure."

"Did Mrs. Landry like it, too?"

"She loved it," I tell him. "But it's funny, we didn't really talk much about the actual book. She told me about her husband, how he used to leave her little love notes to find all around the house."

"That's sweet. I never knew Coach Landry was a softie," Jonny says, smiling.

"*Coach* Landry? You were on the football team?"

"I got kicked *off* the football team." He smirks.

"That tracks," I say, laughing. "But it sounds like they had a really special love story. And I don't know, our conversation got me thinking about how powerful books are. Like, it's not just about the words on the page, but how they make you feel and how they connect to your life. Twenty people could read the same book, and each take away something different."

"So true," he says, nodding. "That's why I was set on having a bookshop as part of the market this year."

He goes on, telling me how he didn't grow up reading much, but that changed when he went to UT Austin and accidentally stumbled into an indie bookstore near campus.

"The store was called Book People, and it was pretty much love at first sight," he says as he makes a left turn. "Two whole floors of books, shelf after shelf. More books than I'd ever seen in my life, each one full of new ideas, new worlds."

"Wait, you went to Texas? That's not easy to get into—I thought you were a punk in high school."

"Turns out punks can still get an almost-perfect score on the ACT." He winks.

"And what do former punks turned multi-millionaires like to read?" I ask. "Wait—don't tell me: books about optimizing workflow, crushing goals, or harnessing your inner CEO?"

That's the kind of book Conor and his bros listen to on their commutes and discuss at work over their green smoothies.

He chuckles. "I mean, sometimes. Nothing wrong with a good self-help book. But I had a professor in college who used to say novels are just self-help books in disguise. Whether it's literary fiction about the AIDS epidemic, a fantasy about a chosen one deciding to be brave, or a mystery where the detective's really solving his own mess—it's all about learning how to be human."

Be still my reader-girl heart. He says it so casually, like he doesn't realize he just spoke directly to my soul.

"Yes! Exactly!" I say, realizing I'm talking with my hands, too excited to keep them in my lap. "It's like you get to live someone else's life for a while, and somehow it makes you understand your own better. It's really beautiful."

"You're really beautiful."

He murmurs the words under his breath, like they slipped out by accident. We're at a red light, and the way he's looking at me, eyes smoldering, makes my stomach flip. And I realize, I don't need a surprise. I don't need anything except for time alone with this man. I still want to sleep with him, but I also want to *talk* with him. Tell him all my stories and hear his. I want to know him, and I want him to know me. I'm tired of hiding.

"Jonny," I say. "There's something else I want to tell you."

"Hold that thought. We're here. Just hang on one second."

He pulls into the parking lot of a gas station and hops out while I wait, wondering what on earth he has planned. He opens my door and helps me out of the truck so I don't have to jump.

"Is there a hidden speakeasy or something around back?" I ask. There's a place in Chicago where you go through what looks like a closet door in a barber shop to get to a secret bar.

"This is just where we're parking," he says, taking my hand in his. "This way."

We're walking toward the town square, and as we get closer, I hear people singing. Are we going Christmas caroling?

My stomach sinks, remembering how it felt at the Christmas tree lighting when I didn't know the words. At least then, there'd been a distraction with his family—now, it will be obvious that I'm an outsider.

"Listen, Jonny...I don't think this is a good idea."

He turns to face me, taking both of my hands in his. "I really don't want to ruin this surprise," he says, glancing in the direction the voices are coming from. "Will you trust me? If we get there and you don't want to stay, I promise, we'll go. Please?"

I take a deep breath and nod.

Jonny looks anxious, which makes me even more nervous. But I can tell this means a lot to him, so I let him lead the way toward the town square and the collective voices singing.

The melody is familiar—"We Wish You a Merry Christmas" —but there's something different about it. The cadence is off. Straining my ears, I hear what they're singing: "We wish you a happy Hanukkah, and a happy New Year."

We turn the corner, and I see what looks like more than a hundred people standing in front of a ten-foot-tall menorah. *A menorah?* In Azalea, Texas?

My jaw drops, and for one confusing, wonderful moment, it's like time stands still.

I glance back at Jonny, who's watching me. He smiles, a little apprehensive, as he says, "Happy Hannukkah, Shira."

Hearing my name on his lips like it's familiar, like it's beautiful, like it's me, makes my eyes well with tears. "What is—? How did—?"

Stunned, I turn back to look at the menorah. The base appears to be made of wood, and the "candles" look like plastic pipes. At the top of each one sits a glass lantern like the kind you'd see on city streetlights. It's incredible—a rustic, handmade work of art.

"Sorry it's a few days late," Jonny says.

"Sorry?" I say, shaking my head. "You did this? For me?"

"It wasn't just me," he says, and I realize there are more familiar faces in the crowd than strangers. Jonny's family is there, along with customers I recognize from the bookstore: Mr. Jenkins and Mrs. Frandsen, the girls who are buddy reading The

Fourth Wing series—even mean old Mrs. Barnes. And the picnic tables around them are covered with an array of Jewish foods: latkes, challah, and gefilte fish. They got some of the holidays wrong, but the sentiment couldn't be more right.

I can barely speak, my eyes so full of tears I'm afraid to blink. "I don't…I can't…"

"You don't have to say anything," Jonny says. "Except maybe the prayer? I know everyone would love to know more about the holiday. About you."

That does it. Tears spill down my cheeks, and I launch myself into Jonny's arms. This man, this town, has taken in a stranger and made her feel like she belongs. And if that's not a miracle, I don't know what is.

CHAPTER 12

JONNY

G rowing up, I spent a lot of time watching my parents together. They're both practical people, not ones for big romantic gestures, but they were always doing little things for each other: Mom making Dad's favorite meal when he'd had a long day, him coming home with flowers for no reason at all, the way they constantly hold hands when they're walking. I soaked it all in, the importance of those quiet acts of kindness. That's the stuff that sticks, I know that.

But every once in a while, you have to throw subtlety out the window, crank the volume to eleven, and make a scene. Go big or go home.

Tonight, that's what I did. And I don't regret it for a second.

More people than I ever expected showed up, a testament to how beloved my parents and siblings are in this town—they invited everyone they know. People of all ages came to mingle, eat, and laugh, learning about a tradition they knew little about. And yes, I love that. But from where I'm standing, it's just one person that matters. Just her smile, soft and amazed, and the way she keeps glancing at me like she can't believe this is happening.

Right now, she's standing at a folding table with my oldest three nieces and nephews and a handful of other kids, showing them how to spin the dreidel. Bianca volunteered to drive all the way into Dallas to pick some up, along with a bunch of other Hanukkah decorations. I lean against a streetlamp, trying to be casual, but really I'm just drinking in the sight of her: the sparkle in her eyes as she coaches Jake through a spin, her smile when he scoops up all the chocolate coins like he's struck gold.

I drift closer, catching her voice as she explains how the Maccabees fought to take back their temple, "which is like a church but for Jewish people," Shira says. The kids lean in, eyes big, chocolate smudges at the corners of their mouths.

"So they were like superheroes?" Jake asks.

"Kind of," she says with a laugh. "Except no capes."

Maggie pipes up. "But how'd the oil last so long?"

"That's the miracle," she tells her. "Sometimes it's right when everything seems the most hopeless that something unexpected happens."

She glances over at me, and my chest gives a weird twinge, like there's a string tied around my ribs and she's tugging on it.

"Well done, son," my mom says, coming up next to me, patting my back.

"I appreciate everyone's help," I say. "It's good for this town to be exposed to other traditions."

She nods. "I agree. But is that why you did this? For the town?"

I shift my weight. "Like I told Dad, no one should feel alone on a holiday."

"So, there's nothing special about this particular someone?" she says, a teasing lilt to her voice.

Oh, there's something special about her. And after tonight, it feels like I'm finally ready to admit that to myself. "Maybe," I say.

Mom laughs softly. "Maybe," she repeats, nodding. "Okay."

Eventually, everyone disperses and goes their separate ways. I help my mom clean up the leftover latkes, then load the tables in Isaac's truck before heading back to find Shira. She's standing about ten yards from the big menorah, her arms folded, staring up at it.

"This must've taken you hours to build," she says quietly, as I come up next to her.

"It wasn't just me," I say. "My dad helped with the design. Isaac helped gather all the materials. My brother-in-law Chad's an electrician, so he did the wiring."

"But you're the one who came up with the idea, right? You're the one who planned everything? You're the one who actually built it?"

I hesitate for a bit, then nod.

"Why?"

"I...came by your place on Sunday evening. Watched you lighting your candles in the window. Not in a creepy way," I add quickly. "I wanted to check on you. You said you weren't feeling well."

"I'm sorry I lied to you," she whispers.

I take her hand, tugging her so she's facing me. "*I'm* sorry that I wasn't someone you felt comfortable sharing this with. I'm sorry that I didn't pay enough attention. I feel awful—"

"It's not your fault," she says, and my shoulders relax. "I didn't know what to expect, coming here. I didn't know how people would react. It felt easier to..."

"Keep this part of yourself private?" I say, and she nods. "But—why were you crying?"

She exhales, her gaze falling from mine. "I guess I didn't realize it would be so hard, being away from family and friends for Hanukkah. Being surrounded by so much Christmas and not having anyone or anything Jewish around."

"I can imagine. It's a lot." She's spending every day in a damn Christmas market, for God's sake.

A small, rueful smile tugs at her mouth. "I don't have anything against Christmas. I actually love a lot of the traditions—growing up, I was so jealous of kids who believed in Santa Claus. When I was in third grade, I rode my bike to the mall and used my allowance to sit on his lap and get a picture."

I grin, imagining a tiny version of Shira climbing on Santa's lap, beaming at the camera.

"But as I got older," she goes on, "I learned to love my own traditions—the candles, the food, the way it feels to be part of something that goes back generations. It's beautiful. It's ours." She swallows. "This year, though, with no one to share it with... I didn't expect to feel so alone."

Her voice catches, and I pull her into a hug. She melts against me, her arms wrapping around my waist and her face pressing into my chest.

"I hate that you've felt lonely," I murmur, my hand sliding up and down her back.

She tilts her chin up, her eyes shining as they meet mine. "I don't feel so lonely now."

"Good." I dip my head, and she rises on her toes like she's been waiting for this all night. When our lips meet, a sigh of relief rushes out of me. I hadn't realized until this moment how nervous I've been about this—if I could pull it off, if it would all come together in time, and most of all, how she'd react. Now all I want to do is wrap my arms tighter around her, kiss her soft and slow, let her know I see her, that she matters.

"There's something else I want to show you tonight," I say when we part, my voice a little rough.

She presses her hips closer, a wicked grin spreading across her face. "Finally."

I bark out a laugh as heat sparks up my spine. "Not that, you perv. It's a *place* I want to show you."

She gives an exaggerated sigh. "Guess I'll have to keep waiting and wondering."

I shake my head, grinning. "You're trouble."

"The town troublemaker himself is calling *me* trouble?"

"Well, I like trouble." Before I can stop myself, I lean in to steal another quick kiss.

But she reaches up and cups my face, holding me there, and the kiss tilts—deeper, slower, her hands sliding into my hair. My brain fogs. I forget the truck, the menorah, the plans, everything but the taste of her. My mouth drifts to the corner of her jaw, down her neck, chasing the soft sound she makes.

Slow down, I remind myself. But that's feeling like a tall order right at this moment.

"I thought you wanted to go somewhere," she murmurs.

"Never mind," I say, between kisses. "It's...not that important a place."

Pulling away, she smirks up at me. "No, no, you've piqued my interest. Can't back out now."

I blow out a breath, running a hand through my hair. "You kiss me like that and expect me to operate a motor vehicle in a responsible manner?"

"Who said anything about being responsible?" she shoots back. "Come on. Take me, Jonny."

Her voice is low and teasing, so damn sexy, and in a heartbeat, I'm ready to slide back into my old rhythm, give her exactly what she's asking for.

Leaning down, I put my mouth right next to her ear. "You want me to take you? Tell me where, when, and how."

"My bedroom. Ten minutes from now. Fast and hard."

"Fuck," I mutter as heat sparks through me. "Have you always been this naughty, Ms. Student Council President? Or is it my bad influence?"

"It's definitely you."

Groaning, I blink hard and force myself to refocus. "Knock it off, Trouble. I've been planning this for days, and it's not something we can do just any night."

"What isn't?"

"This...thing I want to do with you."

She laughs. "You're really good at making everything sound dirty."

"I think that's just your dirty mind." I deliberately take a giant step back and try to adjust myself discreetly. She definitely notices, and a tiny smile creeps over her as she bites her lower lip.

"All right, no need to look so smug," I warn, teasing. Then, in a lower voice, I say, "In all seriousness, though, do you want to come with me? Because I'd really love to share it with you."

I find myself holding my breath, hoping she hears what I'm actually asking. Something I'm not sure I even understand myself.

Her smile fades away as she looks up at me, her eyes big and brown and luminous. "I think I might go anywhere with you, Jonny McKay."

My stomach does a slow somersault. "Well, then. Let's go."

I drive up to the slight rise on the southwest corner of my parents' property, a spot that overlooks the alfalfa fields rolling out toward the tree line and the lights of Azalea beyond. It's a clear night, the kind where the stars feel so close we could almost reach up and scoop them out of the sky with our hands.

"Don't move," I tell her as I park, and she lifts her hands in mock-surrender.

Getting out of the truck, I circle around and open her door. I reach over her, unbuckling her seat belt while she watches, confused. Then I scoop her up in my arms.

"Jonny!" she squeals, kicking her legs.

"Yes, darlin'?"

"I can walk!"

"Sure you can, but you don't need to." With her in my arms, I shut the door with my hip, then carry her around to the bed of the truck. I set her on the edge and keep hold of her with one arm while I pull back the tarp with the other.

It's all set up: blankets, pillows, an extra-thick foam pad I cut down to fit. A little island of softness and warmth under the enormous dome of sky.

I gently set her down onto it, and she pulls her knees into her chest, looking around. "What is all this for?" she breathes.

"There's a meteor shower tonight," I say. "This is the perfect spot to see it."

I climb in on the other side of her and arrange the pillows so we're propped against the cab, our legs stretched out. I pull my mom's big denim quilt over us, then a fluffy down comforter, tucking everything around her like she's precious cargo.

"Just a few more things," I say, tugging a pink knit hat over her head. Then I pull out a pair of fuzzy pink gloves and put them on her hands, tugging each finger into place as she stares at me, eyes wide.

"You always carry a pink hat and gloves with you?" she says.

"Bought 'em earlier today—but really, it's for selfish reasons. See, if you get cold, I'll have to take you home, and I don't want to miss the meteor shower."

Then, I hand her a thermos of hot cocoa. She takes it, lips parting like she's lost the ability to speak. She looks adorably cozy in the hat and gloves, with the blanket tucked under her armpits. Her eyes are shining, her cheeks flushed, little wisps of dark hair escaping the hat.

"God, you're pretty." The words slip out of me before I can stop them, soft and unguarded.

She glances at me, almost dazed. "You know, I already want to sleep with you. You didn't need to do all this."

My chest tightens. I'm not sure which part bothers me more: that she assumes that's my only motivation here, or that she can't imagine she's worth the effort for any other reason. "Maybe that's not what I'm after tonight. You ever think of that?"

Her eyebrows lift. "Then what are you after?"

Truth is, I don't know how to explain it. Maybe it started as a way to prove that I'm different from the way I once was, to see how it'd feel to slow things down for once, but it's become more than that. I know it has to do with the way I felt when I saw her crying in the window, and it grew even stronger tonight when I watched her in the town square. Now I've got all these feelings jumbled up inside me, feelings I've never had before. I can't even begin to untangle them, let alone put them into words.

All I know is that something is shifting, and it has to do with her.

"I'd love to just...hang out tonight," I say eventually. "Would that be okay?"

Her face goes soft. "Of course."

Relief settles on my shoulders. Before she can say anything else, I twist around to the other side and pull out the white bakery box I stashed there. "I thought about buying enough for the whole town, but my mom was so excited about making the food for tonight—"

"It was all wonderful," she cuts in, nodding.

"Yes, but..." I swallow, suddenly nervous. "I also wanted you to have something more traditional."

I hand her the box, and she opens the lid. She stares, her lips parting, but no sound comes out. My heart feels like a hummingbird trapped in my chest. Did I screw this up?

"I—I read that this is a traditional Hanukkah dessert. Sufganiyot, I think?" I stumble a little over the unfamiliar word. "Sorry if I got it wrong—"

"You didn't get it wrong," she says quietly.

"Then...what is it?"

She doesn't answer right away. Instead, she lifts one of the pastries from the box and takes a slow bite, eyes fluttering shut as she chews and swallows. "So good," she says, licking her lips. "My bubbe—my grandma—used to buy these every year. It's wild how food can drop you right back into a memory, like I'm sitting at her dining room table again."

"I know what you mean," I say. "My Grandma McKay used to make shortbread every Christmas—flaky, buttery, basically irresistible. After she died, my sister Bianca started making them, and whenever I eat them, I can practically hear Grandma hassling me to *stand up straight, elbows off the table, and say please and thank you, Jonathan!*"

Laughing softly, she brushes sugar from her gloved fingertips. "It's like every time you make the recipe, you're carrying them forward. The loved ones you lost. Adding your own layer to what they gave you."

"Exactly."

She smiles, holding the pastry out to me. "Want a taste?"

I nod, and she brings the pastry to my mouth so I can take a bite. "Delicious," I say, swallowing. "Kind of like a jelly-filled doughnut."

"You've got a little something," she says, pointing to the corner of her mouth.

I hold her gaze. "You'd better get it for me."

Her eyes glint with mischief as she takes one glove off. Then she leans closer, brushing away the smear of jam at the corner of my mouth with her thumb. But instead of pulling back, her thumb lingers, tracing a slow line across my lower lip. The world goes still.

On instinct, I draw her thumb between my teeth. My tongue finds the sweetness, tasting sugar and her skin. She inhales sharply as my teeth and tongue slide against her thumb, sucking gently before releasing her.

Then she glances up, gasping. "Look!"

I follow her gaze and catch a streak of light cutting across the dark sky. A couple of seconds later, there's another. We huddle closer, my arm around her and her head settling against my shoulder. The night air is cool, but the space between us seems to glow. Every time she spots another shooting star, she points it out, her voice so full of wonder I can't help smiling.

The ache in my chest swells—sweet and heavy. I wish the world could stop, that we could stay in this little bubble of warmth, like we're the only two people in the universe.

The cocoa goes cold. The pastries are forgotten. Above us, the sky keeps spilling its stars, and we stay there wrapped together, two small figures beneath a galaxy of light.

CHAPTER 13

SHIRA

The sun is peeking over the alfalfa fields when I wake up in the back of Jonny McKay's truck, the little spoon to his big one. The air is frigid against my face, but inside the blankets, it's warm and toasty.

Judging by the soft sound of snoring, Jonny's still asleep. And judging by the size of the bulge pressed against my back, I'm going to be one happy woman when he finally lets me unwrap his package. But even though I'll admit to being a little disappointed last night when Jonny asked if we could just "hang out," it ended up being perfect.

The girls won't understand this—I might not even tell them —but once Jonny made it clear we weren't having sex last night, I was able to relax and open up in a way I haven't before. With anyone. We stayed up until nearly two a.m. talking about everything under the sun while we lay under the stars.

Jonny told me about growing up in Azalea, where he's pretty sure his reputation as the "bad apple" of his family began in kindergarten, when he refused to close his eyes during naptime. He wasn't tired, and he didn't have any interest in following rules just because someone told him to. He still doesn't like pointless rules (like why is the speed limit only thirty miles per hour once you get past the city limits?), and he never bothered to try to change people's perception of him.

It wasn't until he left Azalea that he realized how stifled he'd felt growing up, and how free he felt being somewhere else. Like he could reinvent himself—be whoever he wanted in a big city where no one knew about all the mistakes he'd made. He told me how hard it's been coming back, knowing that he's changed, but the way the town sees him hasn't.

I told him I knew something about reinventing myself, too. Only I hadn't wanted to be different; all I wanted was to fit in. Even from a young age, I didn't feel like I belonged with my family. As the only child of two brainiacs—my dad is one of the top economists in the country, and my mom is a district judge —I never felt like I was smart or analytical enough to be worthy of their time or attention.

Even when it came to reading—something all three of us loved—our tastes were drastically different. I preferred losing myself in fictional worlds instead of the dry, academic ones they favored. I think it disappointed them that I read for escape and entertainment, not enrichment. When they looked down on the books I read, it felt like they were looking down on me.

That's why I spent as much time as I could with my Bubbe. She gave the best hugs and told the best stories. She was the only person in the world who made me feel like I was enough, that who I am is exactly who I'm supposed to be. That's why it's been so hard, feeling that weird push and pull of being proud of myself and wanting to hide the parts that are different.

Sharing those stories of our past and the people who made us who we are was oddly intimate. I feel closer to Jonny than I've felt with any other man, and we haven't even seen each other naked yet.

This morning seems like as good a time as any to change

that. It's a brand-new day, and I'm ready for our physical connection to catch up to our emotional one.

When I arch my back and press my butt toward Jonny, I'm not thinking about what Talia would do if she were here; I'm not thinking at all. I'm fully embracing the part of me that's tired of apologizing for who I am, for what I want, and what I need. And what I need right now is Jonny McKay.

I can feel Jonny respond, his hips shifting toward me, and I'm not sorry. Not one bit.

I glance behind me to see if he's awake; his breathing isn't quite as steady, but his eyes are still closed. I press back a little more and swivel my hips. I'm already wet for him, this man who kisses me like it's the main event, who tells me I'm beautiful, who let me talk for hours about my dead grandmother, and who literally made me a miracle with his own two hands.

"Trouble," Jonny hisses as he grinds against me. His lips are on my neck, and his arms wrap tighter around me. "You are nothing but trouble."

"The good kind, I hope."

"The best kind," he mumbles. "Didn't mean to make you sleep in the back of a truck, though. I should've taken you home—sorry about that."

"I'm not." I shift so we're facing each other, lying on our sides in the back of his truck. Our lips find each other, and his kiss is sleepy and sweet and slow. I shift again, trying to wedge my leg between his, desperate to feel him against me.

"Not yet," Jonny says again, still on the edge of sleep.

I groan, frustrated. This man's self-control would be something to admire if I weren't trying to shatter it. Mine, however, is not so strong. A new thought flickers in my mind, something I have *never* done—at least, not in front of anyone else. But I'm kind of liking this new, bolder version of myself.

And if Jonny's not going to help me, then I'll have to take care of myself.

Without breaking the kiss, I shift slightly and bring my hand to the waist of my jeans. I undo the top button and tentatively slip my hand inside.

Jonny's eyes are still closed as he kisses me, deeper with each press of his mouth. I move my hands the way I'd want him to, imagining that it's his fingers teasing, circling, rubbing. My breath hitches as the pressure builds, and Jonny pulls back.

My hand goes still. His pupils dilate as he realizes what I'm doing. "Don't stop on my account," he murmurs. Shivers run down my legs, and I continue. He keeps his eyes locked on mine, like he's more interested in seeing the pleasure wash across my face than looking at what's causing it.

Soon, my breaths are coming faster, my muscles tightening. Jonny dips his head and kisses me, his tongue sweeping against mine as I pick up the pressure and the pace. The tension builds as he kisses me deeper, and then my hand falls limp as I quiver against him and ride the wave until I'm breathless and spent.

"Fuck," Jonny whispers, "that was…" He blows out a breath, his jaw tightening like he's struggling to hold himself back.

Sighing, I stretch out my leg, sliding my toes against his foot.

"Do you want a turn?" I ask, still breathless.

"Hell yes, I do." He closes his eyes, wincing like he's in pain. "But not in the back of a truck off a side road my brother might drive down at any moment. Plus, my mama always says that good things come to those who wait."

I pout. "Yeah, well, my mom says good things come to those who go after them."

Jonny chuckles and wraps his arm around me. "Opposite ends of the same spectrum."

"Maybe that's our problem," I say, snuggling into him.

"Opposites can attract, but they don't really work, not in the real world."

"I'm not so sure about that." He presses a kiss to the top of my head. "Just think about last night. How beautiful was it, bringing our worlds, our traditions, together?"

"It was beautiful," I agree. "Proof that two things together can be greater than each of them is apart."

"I like that."

"How about we put it to the test?" I say, sliding my leg between his, feeling him hot and hard against my thigh.

He lets out a low groan, pulling me close for a second before sighing. "I should get you home," he says. "So you can shower and get ready before you have to open the bookshop."

There's something in his voice I can't read; he feels far away.

"It's early," I say, turning so I can see his face. "The store doesn't open for hours."

His eyes soften as he brushes hair back from my face. "Hours aren't enough time for what I want to do with you."

"You're killing me, Jonny McKay," I say, snuggling closer and fitting myself against him.

I close my eyes and focus on the rise and fall of his chest, the rhythm of our breaths, the way we inhale and exhale. We're not in sync, but we are in harmony. The thought makes me smile— it's like Jonny said about our different traditions coming together to create something beautiful and new. After all, you can't have harmony with two of the same note. People might be like that, too. People like me and Jonny.

He wraps his arms around me, and I let him hold me, dreaming of a way this could work even after December ends.

. . .

I'm literally giddy as I open the bookshop, counting down the minutes until I can see Jonny again. It's wild how in one night I've gone from melancholy *Folklore* Taylor to *The Life of a Show-girl* Taylor, and I'm not mad about it.

There's a steady flow of customers, which helps pass the time, and I spend the day helping them pick out books to gift or purchase for themselves. Around three o'clock, when the lack of sleep starts getting to me, Jonny walks in wearing a secret smile and holding a big cup of coffee.

I'm talking to Mrs. Landry, who dropped by to tell me how excited she is about the town's new menorah. She's saying how sorry she was to miss the lighting last night. It turns out that her college roommate was Jewish, and she has fond memories of the beautiful traditions they shared.

I thank her and tell her that I'll see her tomorrow to talk about her latest read, *The Stolen Life of Colette Marceau*, then try not to run toward Jonny and his much-needed caffeine.

"I thought you could use this," he says, handing me the coffee. "And I could use this."

He leans in to give me a kiss that's meant to be quick but isn't.

"What if I close up early and we play hooky the rest of the day?" I suggest, anxious to continue this behind closed doors.

Jonny playfully tsks. "Remember, patience is—"

"Overrated," I say, cutting him off with a smile and another kiss.

"What do you want to do later?" he asks. I raise my eyebrows and hook a finger through a loop on his jeans. "Other than that," he says.

"We could bring dinner to my place?" I suggest. "Except I bet you don't have delivery around here."

"We have take out. And I could deliver it."

"I'm pretty sure that's how a lot of old pornos start," I tease, adding a little "bow chicka wow wow."

"Calm down, Trouble—I'm just talking about tacos."

"Okay, fine," I say. "If you bring dinner, then I'll be dessert."

Before Jonny can reply, his phone buzzes, interrupting us. "Sorry, it's Kara," he says.

He answers, and I watch as he talks to his little sister, a patient, loving smile on his face. Jonny does so much for everyone in his family—fetching pregnancy cravings for Kara, watching his nieces and nephews, running the market for his dad—it's hard to imagine how the McKays coped so long without him. Or what they'll do once he leaves again.

We haven't talked about what he's going to do once his dad is back on his feet and his sister has the baby, but I imagine he'll leave town again. Not much of a market for start-up businesses in Azalea, but maybe in Chicago?

Chill, Shira. This is what Talia warned me about; flings aren't supposed to involve feelings, just fucking. Except we're not even doing that.

Maybe the woman at the taqueria was right to warn me all those weeks ago. While Jonny may not be the town troublemaker anymore, he's still that restless guy who moves from city to city, trying new ventures, starting things, and moving on before they've even settled—the kind of man who refuses to be pinned down.

And as much as I've tried to be someone else, deep down, I'm still just a girl who wants to be seen and wanted and chosen for who she really is.

"Sorry about that," Jonny says to me after hanging up. "I've got to bring Kara a jar of olives."

"No dilly beans?"

"I brought her three jars yesterday," he says with a crooked grin. "Sunset is around five-thirty, so I'm going to go add a light to the menorah in the town square—I could be at your place by six-thirty?"

"It's a date," I say, fully embracing whatever weird and wonderful thing is happening between us.

When I get home a few minutes after six, Jonny is already there, leaning against my door with a big smile on his face and a brown bag full of tacos.

"Special delivery," he says, holding up the bag. "Did someone order Hanukkah tacos?"

I lift up on my toes to kiss him before letting us in the front door. "How'd you know that's the traditional meal for the fifth night?"

"Sure it is," he says, then tilts his head like he's considering this. "Is there a tradition for the fifth night?"

"Just lighting the candles. Growing up, the first night and the last night were usually the biggest deal—but nothing has ever or will ever top the fourth night this year."

Jonny shakes his head, way too humble for a man who just grand-gestured the hell out of Hanukkah. After the eleventy-billionth time I thanked him last night, he begged me to stop. He keeps saying it wasn't a big deal, but it was. It is.

"Well, maybe we can start a new tradition," Jonny says. "A fifth night fiesta?"

"I like the sound of that." Both the idea of a fiesta and having a tradition with him. As if this is something we could do together year after year.

Over dinner, I tell Jonny about how many people stopped by to wish me a Happy Hanukkah. If they weren't in the town square for the big menorah reveal last night, they'd heard about it and were excited to learn about a new holiday. Only one person actually said it, but I'm pretty sure I'm the first Jewish person most of the people in this town have ever met.

"Now what?" Jonny asks after we clear the plates. "Dessert or candles?"

"Let's do the candles first. Wait here, and I'll get everything ready."

I leave him at the table, then set out the menorah and get the gift I picked out for him earlier. I'm excited to give him the book, but I'm a little nervous to share this ritual with him. It's different than last night with the big crowd and the party atmosphere. Here, in the quiet, with just the two of us, it feels more important. More sacred.

"Thank you for sharing this with me," Jonny says as he watches me put six candles—one for each night, plus the shamash in the middle—from right to left in the menorah.

"Thanks for being here with me."

I take a slow and steady breath, then strike the match. I glance over at Jonny. He looks almost reverent, standing with his hands folded together. I bring the match to light the shamash, then use the candle to light the others, starting with the newest candles and ending with the first.

"*Baruch atah Adonai*," I sing, "*Eloheinu Melech haolam, Asher kid'shanu b'mitzvotav v'tzi'vanu l'hadlik ner shel Hanukkah*." Then I turn to him and say, "Happy Hanukkah."

"Happy Hanukkah," he says, his voice barely above a whisper.

"That's the part that made me cry the other night," I admit.

"The prayer?"

I shake my head. "The Happy Hanukkah at the end. It's something I've always said after the blessing, almost like it's a part of the prayer. But I realized I didn't have anyone to share it with."

"I'm sorry I wasn't here for you," he says, pulling me into his arms.

"You would've been if I'd told you," I say, and I know deep down it's true. "Besides, you're here now—and I have something for you."

I reach behind me and pull out a wrapped gift. Jonny drops his hands. "Wait, I didn't bring anything for you."

"It's okay," I tell him, taking the bow off the present. I consider sticking it on his crotch and making a joke, but instead, I place it on his chest, right over his heart. The more time I spend with him, the more attracted I am to that part of him. "You being here is a gift," I say. "But open yours."

We sit down on the couch, the candles from the menorah glowing behind us. Jonny lays the gift on his lap, looking at it like it's something precious. It's obviously a book, but he opens it with such tender care that I wonder the last time someone did something nice for him instead of the other way around.

"East of Eden," he says, reading the title out loud.

"Have you read it?" I ask.

He shakes his head and turns the book over to read the back cover copy.

"I was thinking about what you told me the other day," I say. "About your professor who said all novels are about learning to be human. This book definitely does that. Technically, it's a retelling of the Cain and Abel story, but it's also about a person's legacy and the struggle between who people think you are and who you choose to be. How much of the past we have to carry, and—"

Jonny kisses me, cutting me off. His hands slide up to cup my cheek, then into my hair. "Thank you," he murmurs. "So much."

"It's just a book," I say, smiling.

"It's not just a book." His eyes meet mine, dark blue and

intense. "It's the fact that you noticed. That you were paying attention to what I said."

My heart stills. "Of course I was."

He kisses me again, slower this time, as if he's trying to tell me something with each press of his lips. It's like he's thanking me for seeing him, for hearing him, for recognizing all the pieces of him he usually hides. It makes me wonder how many people have underestimated him, have only seen the cocky, flirty exterior. How many have overlooked the kind, loyal, generous man underneath?

I want to be even closer to him, not just to chase a fleeting thrill, but to strip away the layers between us. I want him to know how much he's starting to mean to me, to show him the parts of myself that most people don't get to see, either.

"I'm sorry I didn't get you anything," he whispers between kisses.

"I have an idea for something you can give me," I say, taking his hand and pulling him off the couch. "Follow me."

CHAPTER 14

JONNY

7 DAYS UNTIL CHRISTMAS

Shira pulls me into her bedroom, her fingers already at my belt buckle, and I catch her hands, gently redirecting them.

"Hold your horses," I murmur, kissing her. "We're not there yet."

She pulls back, blinking up at me. "Not there yet? Jonny McKay, I have *never* been this forward with a guy in my life, but you're putting on the brakes at every turn. What's going on? If you're not into me, just say so."

The hurt in her voice hits me hard. This is absolutely not how I wanted her to feel, ever. I slide both hands to her waist, pulling her against me. "Does it seem like I'm not into you?"

Her eyelids flutter as she presses into me. "Okay, then what is it? Did I spoil the thrill of the chase by being too obvious?"

"No," I say. "There's something I should probably tell you, though."

Her brow furrows. "Please don't say you have a girlfriend."

I chuckle. "No."

"Or, wait—did you make some kind of vow of celibacy? A purity promise?"

I bark out a laugh. "Absolutely not."

"Then what's going on?"

I tuck a lock of hair behind her ear, trying to think how to explain that just because I'm not taking her to bed doesn't mean I'm not interested. In fact, it's the opposite. But how do you put into words something you don't even fully understand yourself? I want her, but not in the way I usually want things, restless and fleeting. It's a little disorienting, all these feelings and impulses I'm having around her.

Then something occurs to me—a memory from when I was a kid. A lesson I learned during Christmastime many years ago, and something I guess I'm still working on.

"Can I tell you a story?" I ask her.

She huffs, but curiosity flickers in her eyes. "A story?"

"A holiday story. I'm the main character, so you know it'll be good."

That earns a half-laugh, half-sigh. "Fine."

I guide her to the bed, positioning myself with my back against the headboard, and draw her into the space between my legs. She settles there like she belongs, her back against my chest, her hair brushing my jaw. I press my face to the curve of her neck and inhale the mix of her shampoo, perfume, and skin.

She exhales. "All right, get on with it. What's the story?"

"Bossy, I like it," I say, chuckling. "Once upon a time, there was a naughty little boy who loved Christmas morning."

"Sounds familiar."

I lean against the headboard as my fingers tease the bottom hem of her sweater, finding a gap of warm skin between the soft wool and the waistband of her jeans. Her breath quickens.

"You know my dad's a hay farmer, right?" I say, and she nods. "So that means sometimes we had good years, and others were lean years. And when I was growing up, we had some really lean years."

I think back to those times, when I could see the stress in my parents' eyes, hear their whispered conversations at night about how they'd pay the bills.

"But no matter what," I go on, "my parents always made Christmas feel like the best day of the year—and they always made sure there were plenty of gifts under the tree. Most of them were things we needed, like socks, a new coat, notebooks and pencils for school. Practical stuff. But even when times were hard, my parents always made sure we had at least one gift that was just for fun. A little bit of magic."

I slide my hand under her sweater, fingers splaying against the warm skin of her stomach, and she sighs with pleasure.

"Go on," she says, relaxing against me.

I smile. "Every Christmas morning, I was on a mission to find that special gift as fast as possible. I'd hunt for it, tearing through the paper, bows flying, everyone yelling because I was making a mess."

She lets out a quiet laugh. "I can totally see that."

"Then one year, I think I was about twelve, my Grandma McKay—"

"The shortbread one?"

The fact that she remembers makes my smile widen. "That's right. A few days before Christmas, she was over for dinner, and she pulled me aside next to the Christmas tree. She put her hand on my shoulder and said, 'Jonathan, look at all those pretty gifts under that tree. Now, why do you think we take the time to wrap them up? Wouldn't it be easier to just hand them to people unwrapped?'"

"How did you respond?" Shira asks.

"I don't remember—I think I just wanted her to stop talking so I could get some dessert."

She laughs, then her breath hitches as my hand drifts slowly upward, to her ribcage, right below the bottom edge of her bra. I slide my other hand onto her thigh, spreading my palm wide, feeling her soft curves through the denim.

"But my grandma explained that unwrapping the gift is as much a part of the experience as what's inside. The anticipation, waiting and wondering what it could be. She suggested I try taking my time that Christmas and see how it felt."

"And did you?"

"Sure did," I say, nodding. "That Christmas morning, I tried my best to slow down, and it was surprisingly fun. I realized my grandma was right, that I'd been so desperate to get to the thing inside that I'd ignored everything leading up to it. How the anticipation was its own kind of magic."

I press a kiss to the curve of her neck, and she shivers.

"When the next Christmas rolled around," I go on, "I went even slower. Started with the smallest box. Peeled the tape off one corner. Ran my thumb along the creases. I made myself feel the weight of the paper, its texture, and listened to the sound it made when it tore. My siblings were going crazy, telling me to hurry. But I didn't speed up; I just kept unwrapping slower. And slower."

My hand slides up to cup her breast, a feather-light hold, and she arches into me.

"Every year I stretched it more and more," I say, "and I always saved that one special present—my main present—for last. At first, I dragged it out so long I didn't finish unwrapping that last gift until right before Christmas dinner. Then I started saving it for the next day. One year, I waited all the way until New Year's Eve."

My hand is physically aching with the desire to move under her bra, to feel the heat and softness of her breast under my palm. Instead, I let my thumb drift over the fabric as I listen to the quiet hitch in her breathing. Then, ever so gently, my thumb brushes her nipple.

"Jonny," she gasps. "That's a lot of patience."

I laugh, low against her ear. "You have no idea."

She draws a shaky breath. "And now you're applying this same technique to something other than Christmas presents, I take it?"

"That's right." My eyes drift closed as I circle the peak of her nipple, lazy and slow. I may have learned how to slow down with Christmas presents, but not with other important things. I've been in too much of a rush for too long—in business, and in relationships, too. Pushing forward, getting what I want, then putting it behind me.

But I'm not sure if I want to admit to her how careless I've been in the past, so I say, "I'm trying to remember that the anticipation is part of the magic."

She sighs. "Well, you better not wait to unwrap *me* until New Year's Eve, because I'll be gone by then. If you don't get moving, this holiday fling is going to expire before it even starts."

Her words send a twinge through my chest. *Holiday fling.* Yeah, I guess that's really all it can be. She's going back home to Chicago. I'm staying here until Kara's had the baby and Dad's released to full activity. After that, I have no idea where I'll end up. Whatever happens between Shira and me, it should be simple. Clean. No strings.

So why does my stomach feel like it's hollowing out?

Trying to shake that off, I lower my mouth until my lips brush the hollow of her ear. "Don't worry. It'll be worth the wait."

"So cocky."

"Confident," I correct, pressing a kiss to the curve of her neck. "Because I know I'll deliver."

She lets out a soft, incredulous laugh. "Oh, yeah? And I'm supposed to take your word for it?"

"Nah. Just pay attention to how you feel when I touch you."

I wrap my hand fully over the cup of her bra as my other hand slides up her inner thigh. She melts against me, proving me oh-so-right.

"That final gift," she says, her voice coming out in a rush. "The one you'd wait to open?"

My mouth grazes down her neck. "Mmm-hmm?"

"I'm feeling a little bad for it, being teased for days. Must've been torture."

"You want to talk about torture?" I groan softly, thinking back to this morning. "Let's talk about that little stunt you pulled in the truck."

"What stunt?" She rolls her head to the side, and I take full advantage, sliding my mouth across her skin, tasting, nipping gently.

"Making me watch you touch yourself."

"You could've joined in. You still can."

I slide the hand I've got wrapped around her thigh upward until it's between her legs. "Like that?"

"*Yes*," she breathes. "You're making me lose my mind, Jonny."

"At least we're even, then." I start to move my hand away, but she catches it and holds it against her.

"Please."

The desperation in her voice nearly unravels me. Never in my life have I held off this long, and part of me can hardly believe I'm actually doing it. But another part wants to savor this as long as possible—the tension, the wanting, the closeness.

But goddamn it, I'm so hard it almost hurts, and if she's

feeling a fraction of that, she's teetering on the edge of her own agony.

"All right," I whisper. "Let me make you feel good."

Slowly, I unbutton her jeans, then slide my hand inside them, but over her panties. She makes a growling sound in her throat and grabs my hand, sliding it *under* her panties.

My brain glitches. "Fuck."

"I'd love to," she says, "but apparently that's off the table for tonight."

Her legs fall open as she slides my hand lower, my mind going blank so all I register is heat and softness and *holy hell, she's wet.*

"Can I take advantage of your hand for a few minutes?" she murmurs.

Somehow, I gain control of my voice, though it comes out strained. "Yeah, I'll allow it."

She guides my hand lower, right where she wants it, showing me how she likes to be touched. Circling and teasing as she arches against me, her breathy sighs making my entire body go hot.

"I want your fingers inside me," she whispers, moving my hand to do just that, then sliding my fingers out again, slick and soft, and I swear to God I don't remember why I had this stupid plan to *wait* in the first place. I'm sitting on a bed with a woman who is so damn ready to go, who's made her desires crystal clear, so why the fuck am I not tossing her on her back and burying myself inside her right this second?

"Jonny," she gasps, snapping me out of that.

"Yes, love?" The endearment slips out before I can think.

"I'm so close."

Her whole body is tight, taut, electric, and suddenly nothing matters but giving her exactly what she's craving. Her hand falls away from mine, and I take over, mirroring the movements she was guiding me through, letting her breathing tell me if I'm on the right track. She's starting to squirm a little, and I wrap my other arm around her torso, pulling her flush against me. As soon as I do, she relaxes, like all she needed was to know I've got her.

And then, fuck me, somehow I'm pressing a kiss to the top of her head, whispering against her hair as her breathing goes ragged. *That's right. I've got you. Let go, baby. Let go.*

My chest is constricting, a low, throbbing pressure that has nothing to do with the heat between us. It's more than arousal. More than desire. This is something else. Something that makes me want to pull her close and never let go. An urge to protect her, claim her—not in a controlling way, but like she's irreplaceable and precious and *mine.*

The word echoes in my head, soft but insistent: *mine, mine, mine.*

She shivers against me, legs beginning to tremble. "So close," she whispers.

But I can still feel the hesitation lingering in her body, holding her back, and I bring my lips to her ear, voice low, reverent, spilling out words I hadn't even planned:

"You know what present I always saved for last? Not the biggest box, not the shiniest paper. It was the one that felt like it had a secret inside. The gift I never even dared to hope for, the one I was almost scared to open because I wanted it so badly. Shira, that's you. You're like that final gift. You make me want to slow down, savor every aching moment. Because I know, without a doubt, that you'll be worth every second of the wait."

And then she breaks—back arching, legs tightening, letting out a wild sound that vibrates against me. I hold her as she rides it out, murmuring low reassurances until she finally goes limp, her body melting into mine.

I press a soft kiss to the curve of her shoulder, letting her warmth settle against me. And then all I feel is the slow, all-consuming, totally foreign and downright terrifying sensation of never, *ever* wanting to let her go.

We spend the rest of the evening entirely on her bed—eating ice cream while watching a Hanukkah movie on the Hallmark channel (one of only a few, she tells me).

When it's over, we stay there curled up on the bed facing each other, foreheads resting together, eyes half-closed. Talking and laughing, sharing stories from childhood, high school, and college. Fingers trace lazy patterns along arms and shoulders, lips brushing in soft, lingering kisses. Time slips by, hours feeling like minutes.

It's well past midnight when I reluctantly peel myself away and get up. She walks me to the door, her hair a little messy, her clothes rumpled. I can't help myself from putting my arms around her and pulling her into a long, tight hug, just breathing her in.

I want more of this.

The thought hits me like a fist to the stomach. She's leaving on Christmas Day, and whatever this is between us has a ticking clock. A holiday fling, like she said. And that's great. That's fine. Except...*shit.* There's that twinge in my chest again, like I want to open up my ribcage and tuck her inside, keep her safe, keep her warm. Make her mine.

I take a step back, forcing myself to loosen my grip, but I can't stop my hand from brushing the curve of her waist as I let go. She looks up at me, all sleepy-eyed and soft, and my heart stutters. *One week left.*

"What are you doing tomorrow evening?" I ask.

"I don't know, what am I doing, Jonny?"

The teasing note in her voice makes me grin. "Hopefully,

you're joining me for the Great McKay Gingerbread Decorating Party?"

"Um, sure. I don't think I've ever decorated gingerbread before, but it sounds really...cute."

I snort. "It's definitely *not* cute. We've been doing this since we were kids, and every year it starts out wholesome until someone gives a gingerbread lady a pair of gumdrop boobs, and someone else pulls the legs off a gingerbread man and names him Lieutenant Dan."

She laughs. "By *someone* and *someone else,* do you mean you and you?"

"Maybe..." My hand sneaks out and wraps around her waist, pulling her against me again because I already miss her feel of her. "But my siblings are just as bad in their own ways. Brace yourself."

"If I can handle you, I bet I can handle them."

"That'll be the sixth night of Hanukkah, right?" I say, and she nods. "Could you bring your menorah? We can light the candles there."

"You sure? I don't want to take over your family's tradition."

"Believe me, it'll be welcomed by everyone. A little moment of serenity in the chaos."

She smiles, soft and almost shy. "Okay. Can't wait."

I pull her close again, pressing my lips to the top of her head because apparently that's something I can't keep from doing around her. "Me neither."

After one last goodbye kiss, I head outside and into the cool night, a goofy smile tugging at my lips. My mind drifts, remembering the warmth of her, the softness of her skin, the sound of her laugh. I can still smell her on me, and I start thinking about the next time I'll get to be with her, how I'll hold her, kiss her, make her laugh again.

When I get in the truck, I close the door, lean back against the headrest, and close my eyes. As I do, her face flashes in my mind: big brown eyes, flushed cheeks, soft lips. Groaning, I shake my head.

I am so fucked.

CHAPTER 15
SHIRA
6 DAYS UNTIL I HAVE TO LEAVE

For the first time since we opened, I'm closing the store early today. At least, I'm trying to. Just one customer is standing in my way—an older woman in her sixties with hair that resembles a football helmet, who seems intent on reading the back cover copy of every book in the store.

She's been telling me, "Just one more minute, dear," for the last thirty minutes. I haven't wanted to push, but I've got a gingerbread decorating party to get to.

I'm hovering as close as I can without being too obvious when Jonny walks in wearing a sweatshirt with "Santa's favorite" written across the chest in white block letters. He looks every bit the Fun Uncle, and I marvel at the multitudes of this man. This misunderstood millionaire with the self-control of a saint, who positively lit me up with his magic fingers the other night.

His smile falters when he clocks the stress on my face. I shrug toward the woman and mouth, "She won't leave."

Jonny nods in an "I've got this" way and rolls his shoulders before coming around to approach the woman.

"Hello, Mrs. Matthews," he says. "Not sure if you noticed, but the bookstore is closing early today."

"One more minute," she says, reaching for another book from the shelf. Before she can read the back, Jonny gently plucks it from her hands and places it back on the shelf.

"I'm afraid time's up, ma'am. But the shop will open again at ten a.m. tomorrow," he says, his voice kind, but firm.

Mrs. Matthews glances up at him. "My goodness," she says, holding her hand up to her chest, looking affronted. "I can't imagine what your poor mother would think about you rushing a lady out like this."

"She raised me to be polite, ma'am," Jonny says, just the slightest smirk playing on his lips. "And punctual."

She huffs and wraps her coat tighter around her before walking toward the door. I follow behind her, barely holding back a smile. Before she walks out, she turns to me and whispers a warning. "If you're smart, you'll stay away from that boy. He's a bad influence."

Her words light a fire in my belly. I'm tired of people thinking they're better than Jonny, talking badly about him as if he hasn't grown up in the last decade. "He may be a bad influence," I say, "but he's really good in bed."

I shut and lock the door, leaving the woman staring at me with her mouth ajar. Jonny barks out a laugh and waves at Mrs. Matthews until she walks away.

"Too much?" I ask.

"Just right," Jonny says, kissing me. "Now are you ready to get your gingerbread on?"

As we drive toward the edge of town where Jonny's family farm is, I look out the window at the giant bales of hay every hundred feet or so. There's something comforting about the symmetry of it.

"Is there a reason the bales are spaced out so evenly?" I ask.

"It's just how the baler works." He gestures out the window like he can see the tractor in his mind. "They cut the alfalfa with a swather first, then it lies there to dry for a couple of days. Then they come through with a baler, which rolls it up inside the chamber. Once the bale hits a set diameter—usually five feet or so—the machine automatically wraps it in netting, pops it out back, and you keep going. Wherever the baler spits one out, that's where it stays."

"Interesting."

"They're still kind of green when they're first rolled," he adds. "If you stack them up before they're dry, they'll mold or even combust. By the time they're that sun-bleached tan you're seeing now, they've cured enough to store or haul off to the farmers."

"Huh," I say. "That makes sense—but I wasn't expecting the answer to be so...logistical."

Jonny laughs. "I can come up with a more interesting story if you want. Something about aliens, maybe the farmers are using the patterns to send a message. Like braille, but with bales of hay."

"That would actually make a cute children's book," I tell him. "Finding fantastical reasons for the simplest things. Maybe that could be your next venture?"

"I'll stick with reading books. Let the more talented people write them and the more beautiful people sell them."

He flashes me a grin, slowing the truck as we approach a wide road with stone pillars on either side. It's decked out for Christmas, with white twinkle lights, green garland, and big red bows. The black metal gate is open, and as we drive through, I notice the words "McKay Ranch" spelled out on top.

"Wow."

It was dark the other night when Jonny brought us here, and we must have come in and left through a back way. I had a feeling the McKays had a lot of property, but I wasn't expecting it to be this stately.

"This land has been in my family for generations—goes back to my great-great-great-grandfather," he says. "My grandad's the one who built the house I grew up in. My parents made a few upgrades, but it's mostly the same."

"Amazing to have such roots and history in one place."

He nods, eyes on the road. "I used to resent it. Felt like those roots were trying to trap me here. Pin me down."

My mind drifts back to my own history and scattered roots, entire generations and their stories lost during World War II. Even my DNA couldn't tell me more specifics—the 23andMe test I took just came back, "Ashkenazi Jew." And when it comes to my own family, after my parents divorced and Bubbe died, I felt untethered.

"But roots can be so grounding," I say. "Knowing where you come from. Always knowing you have a safe place to land."

"Yeah," Jonny says, his voice thick with emotion. "I don't think I really appreciated it until I came back." He clears his throat and then says, "Let's get in there; the animals are waiting."

We walk inside the two-story ranch house and are instantly greeted with the best kind of chaos. Christmas music is playing, the air is filled with the scent of cookies baking and firewood burning, and it's hard to tell who is more excited to see Uncle Jonny—the kids or the two golden retrievers circling us underfoot.

"Samson, down," Jonny says. "Delilah, off. Come here, you."

He scoops Maggie up with one arm and gives her several loud kisses on her cheek. She squeals and wraps her arms around his neck, hugging him tight.

"Finally!" Jake yells, charging toward us. "We've been waiting FOREVER AND EVER for you!"

Jonny gives the boy a noogie. "Never too young to learn about the virtue of patience. Trust me," he says, looking back at me. "Good things come to those who wait."

Good, lord. I clench my thighs together, wishing Jonny's family wasn't around so he could give me the whole tour, starting with his bedroom.

I follow Jonny toward the living room, where overstuffed couches are angled toward the massive stone fireplace, a roaring fire inside. Family photos line the walls, and I hope I'll get a chance to take a closer look later.

"Jonathan!" a deep voice bellows. "You'd better introduce me to that young lady of yours."

Jonny turns to me, a wry smile on his lips. "Ready to meet my dad?"

Nerves bubble through me. "Uh, sure."

He leads me over to the big arched space between the kitchen and living room, where his dad is stretched out on an oversized floral recliner. He's sturdy and broad like his sons, with a six-inch graying beard and a cast on his right foot up to his knee.

"Dad, this is Shira Schwartz," Jonny says, then to me, "Shira, this is my father, Jed McKay."

"Hello, Mr. McKay, nice to meet you," I say, coming closer so I can shake his hand. He's decked out in a fuzzy green sweater that looks like the Grinch's scowling face.

"Likewise." He takes my hand in his as he glances up at Jonny. "Now get out of here, son. I'm talking to my new friend Shira."

Jonny grins and mouths, *Good luck*, before walking away.

Mr. McKay refocuses on me, still holding my hand between his. "You know, everyone in this house has been talking about you. I hear you're smart, hard-working, and pretty damn brave, too."

My cheeks flush. "Oh, I don't know about brave."

"Well, what else would you call it?" he says. "You moved to a tiny town where you don't know a soul and set up a bookstore where there's never been one before. I'd call that brave. And I bet your parents are right proud. I would be."

Before I can think of a reply, he squeezes my hand and lets go. Then he nods at the kitchen, where Jonny disappeared to help his mom with the cookies.

"You're also brave to take on that one. If he treats you wrong, you come talk to me, you hear? I'll set him straight." He smiles, a cheeky grin that reminds me of Jonny. "Now you go on and have fun, Shira. Pleasure to meet you."

His words are still echoing in my mind as I head back into the kitchen. It's crazy, but I feel more supported by Jonny's family in the short time I've known them than I have by my own family since Bubbe died.

The McKays' kitchen is impressive—it's at least three times the size of my entire studio apartment. A big island divides the cooking space from a wooden table big enough to seat more than a dozen people. Baking sheets stacked with bare gingerbread cookies are set in the middle, surrounded by colorful bowls of candy toppings and tubes of icing.

"Shira!" Jonny's mom sounds genuinely excited to see me. "Don't you look beautiful. I'm so happy you could join us."

"Thanks so much for having me," I say, hugging her, and handing her a wrapped gift—a cookbook I thought she might like. "You look so festive," I tell her. She's wearing a Santa hat and a red apron that says "Head Elf."

A realization settles over me, and I slowly look around the room, suddenly aware that everyone, even the baby, is wearing an "ugly" Christmas outfit.

I glance down at my own navy sweater and the Star of David necklace I no longer bother to tuck in, wishing I could shrink into myself and disappear. I obviously don't have an ugly Christmas sweater, but I could've come up with something if Jonny had given me a heads-up.

He's nowhere to be seen, but from the screeching giggle of the kids in the next room, I know I won't have to look far to find him.

"You do look really pretty," Bianca says from over by the counter.

"Too pretty," Annabel, Jonny's sister-in-law, agrees. She's got a wicked smile on her face, and I feel like I'm about to get pranked.

"We got you a present!" Maggie bursts out, beaming. "It's a sweater!"

Bianca rolls her eyes. "If you ever want to keep a secret, don't tell this one." She hands a wrapped box to Maggie, who brings it to me, suddenly shy.

"This is so sweet," I say. "Thank you."

"Don't thank us yet," Annabel says. "We had to get creative."

I take my time peeling back the paper, thinking of little Jonny slowly unwrapping the gifts that meant the most to him. My cheeks flush, recalling the way he's been slowly unwrapping me, and I focus back on this thoughtful gift from his sisters. There's a white box inside, and I lift the lid to see a royal blue sweater with a felt dreidel sewn on the front. The Hebrew letters are stitched crookedly in white thread, silver and blue sequins sparkle everywhere, and tiny white pompoms wobble along the collar. It's lopsided and messy—and completely perfect.

I'm speechless, flooded with warmth and appreciation for the entire McKay family, who have once again shown me that being different doesn't mean that I can't belong.

"I hope it's okay," Bianca says, misreading my quiet.

"It's better than okay," I tell her, my eyes welling with tears. "It's perfect, thank you. I really love it."

I excuse myself to go to the bathroom and trade the cashmere sweater my mom sent for Hanukkah with the new one. I stare at my reflection in the mirror. The sweater really is ugly, but it's also the most beautiful thing I've ever seen.

By the time I return to the kitchen, the cookie decorating has already commenced. I was only gone a few minutes, but there's already more icing on the kids' faces than on the actual cookies.

"What've you got there?" Isaac says, taking a seat next to Maggie.

"No!" the little girl shouts. "I want Shira to sit next to me!"

"Well, okay, then," Isaac says, standing back up. He holds his hands out, as if presenting me with the seat. "It seems you've captivated all the McKays."

I flash him a grateful smile before taking the seat next to Maggie. "Looks yummy," I say, admiring the blue blob of icing on her gingerbread man.

"It's Cookie Monster," she says, looking proud of her work of art.

Jonny takes a seat on the other side of me and gives me a quick lay of the land. "Basically, there are no rules," he says. "But the more sugar, the better, and this crew tends to be more naughty than nice..."

"Got it." I snap an arm off my first gingerbread man.

Bianca laughs and takes a seat at the table across from me. "Don't screw this one up, Jonny. We like her."

"We love her!" Maggie says, giving me a hug that gets icing all over my new sweater. My heart swells with love for this little girl and her whole big, messy family, who have made me—a Jewish girl from Chicago—feel not just welcome but wanted.

The conversation flows as we decorate, bouncing from topic to topic. One minute they're arguing over which quarterback got "robbed" at the game last week, and the next they're gossiping about the mayor and the church deacon who apparently had a shouting match at the grocery store. I can't follow all the details, and I still don't know what a deacon is or what they do, but my sides hurt from laughing.

We take turns presenting our gingerbread cookies. Mine aren't the best, but they aren't the worst, either. I started by making Captain Hook, then cobbled together Peter Pan and Tinker Bell. Jonny made a Rabbi with some guidance from me, complete with a kippah on his head and a tallit around his shoulders. Then, he made Santa Claus wearing a speedo and Mrs. Claus in a bikini.

Bianca made her cookies bikini-clad, too. She used two different cookies to showcase the same "beach babe" from the front and behind. She used the arms of another cookie to give the cookie a bigger butt with a thong, and as Jonny promised, used gumdrops on the other cookie to give her boobs.

Isaac made a bunch of murder victims, using red icing as blood where the arms and legs were broken off. But the most impressive cookie came from Mrs. McKay, who created a whole series of bodybuilders, complete with muscles and hairy chests made from chocolate sprinkles.

Mr. McKay stayed in his recliner near the edge of the kitchen, but the grandkids kept running back and forth to feed him scraps of their discarded cookies.

I breathe it all in: the teasing, the chaos, the easy laughter, the way everyone includes me without a second thought. I've never felt this way before, carried in a tide of love I didn't even know I was missing.

When Jonny's hand squeezes my thigh under the table, it sends a spark all the way through me. I look up at him, expecting to see him sending a naughty grin my way. Instead, his eyes are fond, almost gentle, like he's just happy I'm here. I'm happy I'm here, too, and I get the strangest sensation that I'm exactly where I'm supposed to be.

It's confusing since I also can't wait to get back home to my friends in Chicago. If the Hanukkah candles were like birthday ones that you could blow out and make a wish, I would wish that the map could be reorganized, that Chicago could butt up against Azalea so I could somehow go home without leaving here.

After all the cookies have been decorated or devoured, Mrs. McKay pops a few pizzas in the oven. While they cook, she asks if I brought my menorah.

Everyone gathers around, and I let Jake and Maggie help me put the candles in. I light the shamash but hesitate before starting the prayer.

I look around at this beautiful family who opened their home and their hearts to me, who haven't just shared their holiday tradition with me, but invited me to share mine with them.

"This is the shamash," I tell them, holding the candle up for them all to see. "It's the most important candle on the menorah because it's the one you use to light the others. And I want to thank you all for being a shamash to me. Each one of you has brought me so much light this holiday."

Jonny steps closer behind me and rests his hand on my shoulder. His presence grounds me, and I light the rest of the candles and recite the blessing. After I reach the end of the prayer and say, "Amen," Jonny brings his lips to my ear and whispers, "Happy Hanukkah, Shira."

His words wrap around my heart, and I know he's thinking of my tears on the first night when I was all alone, the opposite of tonight.

I turn to thank him with a quick kiss, but the emotion shimmering in his eyes stops me. We hold each other's gaze, and for one beautiful moment, I consider the miracle of Hanukkah and wonder if there's a way, if there's a world, where I could hold on to this feeling.

Not just for the month, but for forever.

CHAPTER 16

JONNY

Driving back toward town, I can't stop sneaking glances at Shira. Tonight was unexpectedly perfect. She navigated my family like a pro, chatting with my parents, teasing my siblings, letting my nieces and nephews cling to her. But it wasn't just her ease with everyone—it was what that did to me, watching her. Seeing how she was able to join in while also being completely herself...somehow, it made me feel more at ease, too.

Plus, every member of my family—at least, the ones old enough to speak—found a moment to corner me and tell me how much they like her. The problem is she's leaving soon. For the first time in my life, I'm not looking forward to Christmas.

"What?" she says, catching me staring.

"Nothing." I shake my head. "Just that you seem way too far away over there."

Smiling, she folds up the middle console, then unbuckles and scoots over until she's right next to me. I wrap an arm around her shoulders as she buckles the middle seat belt.

"Much better," I murmur. "How are you holding up after all that?"

"It was a lot of fun." She snuggles against me. "Your family's great—I bet they're going to miss you when you leave again."

"Maybe, yeah." I shift in my seat, a little uncomfortable—both with the thought of staying and the thought of leaving again. "You know, I've been thinking about something."

"Tell me."

"It was something you said when we were at the bar last week. About how I have all this start-up energy and no long-term follow-through."

She sucks in a breath. "Oh. I...sorry, that was kind of a shitty thing for me to say."

"No, you're right. That's how I've been for a long time. But lately, I've been craving something different. Like, a bigger project that I can really sink my teeth into, where I can leave my mark. Something more permanent. I'm just not exactly sure what that looks like yet."

"What lights you up inside?" she says. "What gets you excited?"

You.

The thought flares in my mind, and I quickly snuff it out. That's not at all what she meant. My chest is doing that thing it seems to do around her, that almost-painful tug that makes me want to get closer to her even though she's right next to me.

"I've loved seeing the town come together for this holiday market this year," I say.

"Do you think you'll run it again next year?"

"Nah," I say, shaking my head. "My dad'll be healed up by then. Besides, the building will probably be torn down in a few months anyway."

"Really?" she says, surprised. "That's too bad. In Chicago, a cool industrial place like that would totally be turned into fancy loft apartments or something."

"Nobody's going to invest in something like that in a place like Azalea, though. They'd have to have some serious vision."

"I mean, you could do it."

I pause. "What do you mean?"

"You could be that investor. If you wanted. Show this town how lucky they are to have you."

The idea of stepping into that role, shaping the future of a corner of this town...it's interesting. But then my old instincts resurface, the part of me that knows this town will never see me any differently than they already do. As much as I've enjoyed spending time with my family, being Fun Uncle Jonny, I still worry that I could start to feel suffocated.

"Not sure how people around here would feel about that," I say finally. "You've been warned off me what, a half-dozen times?"

Her hand settles on my thigh, making my pulse skip. "Maybe I'm tired of caring what other people think."

"Careful, Trouble," I murmur as her hand slides up my thigh. "I'm driving."

"Then keep your eyes on the road," she says, her voice teasing as she squeezes my thigh. "You know what I've been thinking about?"

"Tell me."

"I wonder if maybe all that troublemaking you did as a teenager was just a way to show everyone you were different."

I never really thought of it like that before, but it's true. Once I left for college, all that bad behavior stopped. I started getting good grades. I had zero interest in anything even remotely illegal.

"Maybe," I say.

She leans her head against my shoulder, exhaling. "When I first came here, I was hiding pieces of myself because I thought people here wouldn't understand, or they'd judge. But you helped me see I didn't have to hide. And when I finally opened up, your family, this town...they embraced me." She pauses, her hand warm on my thigh. "I bet you can do the same, Jonny. Show them who you are now. And even if some of them never fully see or understand...if you know who you are, does it really matter what they think?"

Her words loosen the knot of self-doubt I've carried for years. Not all the way, but a little. She came here so scared to show her authentic self, and it's been inspiring to watch her open up. Could I do that, in my own way?

"We'll see," I say softly, then clear my throat. "What's next for you—going back to work for Conor? By the way, I'm not sure whether to send him a fruit basket to thank him for sending you here or punch him in the throat for expecting it of you."

She laughs, lifting her head off my shoulder. "Well, he owes me a promotion to Senior Project Manager."

"Is that what you want to do?"

"It's what I've been working toward for a while."

We pass the textile mill on my left. Ahead, the stoplight changes to red, and I ease the truck to a stop. I glance over at her. "Yeah, but...is it what you want?"

Her eyes lift to mine, big and brown and shining. "One thing I've learned in life is that you don't always get what you want."

The quiet ache in her voice punches straight through my chest. "Tell me what you want, love, and I'll make sure you get it."

And I mean it. In this moment, I would tear the world apart to give her whatever she asked.

Her gaze drops, lashes lowering as her fingers ghost over the fly of my jeans. "Right now..." she whispers, "what I want is you."

Her touch sends a spark racing down my spine. She strokes

the seam of my jeans again, slow and deliberate, and heat rises sharp and sudden.

"I feel the same," I say, my voice roughening, "but that's probably obvious."

"I could do something about that," she says, her hands moving to my belt buckle.

"Shira..." Her name is a warning and a plea all at once. I'm trying to hold on to my last thin thread of control, but she's burning through it fast. Thank God there's no one else at the intersection.

"Keep an eye out for other cars," she murmurs as her fingers work the buckle loose. And then she's easing my zipper down, sliding her hand inside my boxers, and wrapping it around me. Her hand is small and warm and so fucking soft, it's like heaven.

I let out a low groan. "This is...really unsafe."

"Tell me to stop, then," she says, teasing.

But I find I have no words, especially as her hand starts to move, slowly sliding up and down, teasing me at the tip.

"Oh, fuck," I breathe. I'm aching for her, trying to hold myself back from thrusting into her hand. Closing my eyes, I let my head drop against the headrest. The light turns green, but there's no way in hell I'm moving now.

A flicker of memory: me at sixteen or seventeen, fumbling and selfish, chasing the high, leaving behind a trail of disappointed girls and a hollow feeling in my chest. I thought I'd changed in adulthood, but did I really? For years, I've been in such a rush, never taking the time to build anything real.

Until her.

Yes, I want Shira like I've never wanted anyone before. But it's more than chemistry, more than desire. For the first time, it doesn't feel like I'm rushing into this moment. It feels like I'm arriving—like together, we're stepping onto something solid, a foundation built on care, affection, and trust. She's the one who made me want to try. The one who made me want to be better than I've been.

And now I'm absolutely certain that moving forward will only deepen what's already there between us.

"We're not doing this here," I grit out.

She releases me and looks up. "But we're doing it *somewhere*, right?"

I drag a hand over my face, trying to catch my breath. "Yes. Just not in the front seat of my dad's truck at an intersection in the middle of town."

The light's turned red again, giving me time to think.

"My place is way too far away, so pull over," she says. "Do you still have that mattress back there? Or you can just take me in the back seat," she teases. "That's what everyone's been warning me of, right? Maybe I want to see what all the hype's about."

Her words are playful, but they land like a dare. I lean closer, my mouth at her ear, my voice dropping. "That was a long time ago. I've got better moves now."

"You think you can make me forget all those rumors?"

"I think I can make you forget your own name."

Her eyes flare with heat. "So cocky," she whispers, but before I can say anything, she adds, "I know. Confident."

"Damn right." I reach down and zip up my jeans, still hard, still aching, but focused now.

"Where are we going?" she asks. The light turns green again, and I hit the gas.

"Hold on."

I crank the wheel in a fast U-turn, tires squealing, then head back toward the textile building.

. . .

I unlock the back door, and we rush inside. As soon as I've locked it behind me, my hands are on her, lifting her as she wraps her legs around my waist.

"Are we done being patient?" she says. "Because I really, really want you."

"Fuck patience. I think we've earned this."

We collide, mouths and hands moving fast, hungry. Her head rolls back as I kiss her neck, my hands roaming, one sliding under her sweater, the other inside her pants to cup her ass.

"I want you," she repeats, more urgently. "Right here, right now."

I kiss her, hard on the mouth, then say, "I'm not fucking you against the wall, Shira."

"Please?"

I thrust instinctively, and she moans. "Like that?" I growl.

"Yes."

But my brain is catching up to my body now. This is better than the truck, but it still isn't how I want it. Later, we'll do hard and fast. But this first time, I want to taste every inch of her, trace every curve, see her eyes gazing up at me when I come inside her.

I want this, all of it, to matter.

"Follow me," I say, setting her down.

I lace our fingers and lead her through the darkened market, our footsteps echoing. As soon as we enter the bookshop, she's gripping my shirt, her mouth finding mine like she's starving.

I back her into a bookcase, one hand sliding under her thigh, lifting her leg high against my hip. Her lips part beneath mine, and I cradle her jaw with my other hand, holding her there while I kiss her deeper.

"Was this your plan all along?" she gasps between kisses. "To take me against the romance shelf?"

Hazy, I glance up and see the rows of books, the pink hand-written sign saying FIND YOUR LOVE STORY. "Is that what you want, baby?"

"I could be into it."

I press her against the bookcase, just enough to rattle it. "Glad we tightened those locky spinny pieces."

She laughs, breathless. "If you topple any of these shelves, you're putting them back together."

Another thrust against her, a hard kiss on the mouth. "Good thing I'm a handyman."

"Handsy, more like it."

Laughing, I lift her as she wraps her legs around me. I'm not about to undo all the work she put into this place because I'm too eager and greedy to slow down.

I carry her toward the register and set her on the counter, both of us breathing hard. Her hair's a mess, her lips kiss-swollen, that ridiculous handmade sweater all rumpled. I love seeing my polished, put-together girl unraveling like this. Makes me desperate to watch her fall apart, to know that I'm the cause.

"Wait here," I tell her.

She makes a growling sound in her throat, tugging me closer.

"I'll be right back," I promise, brushing my lips over hers before pulling away.

I jog back through the silent market, heart hammering, grabbing quilts from a booth, a few candles, and a box of matches from another. When I return to the bookshop, she's still perched on the counter, legs swinging, teeth worrying her bottom lip.

"So in addition to defiling your town's Christmas market, you're also a thief?" she teases, voice husky.

Grinning, I say, "I'll pay double for everything tomorrow."

I spread one quilt across the rug, then another on top, folding it back like a bed turned down. I light the candles and set them around, golden pools of light flickering up the shelves, dancing off the spines of books. The space feels less like a pop-up shop now, more like a secret, magical library created just for us.

When I glance back at her, she's watching me with a soft smile, eyes shining. "Who'd have guessed the town trouble-maker's a romantic?"

I walk over to her, step between her knees. "You're the one who said I should show the real me."

Her smile widens as her hands come to my shoulders, then slide up into my hair, her fingernails rasping against my scalp.

"I love that," I sigh.

"Hmm?"

"Your hands in my hair."

She continues stroking my hair as I kiss the soft spot beneath her jaw, then down her neck, nipping with my teeth and soothing with my lips. I'm lost in her, the feel of her, the taste, my entire body humming with need—and another sensation that's softer, warmer, deeper. Unfamiliar. Terrifying.

"I've been thinking about what you said the other day," she says as my mouth moves to the other side of her neck. "About how you'd wait and wait to open your last present."

"Mmm," I murmur between kisses. "Yeah?"

She pulls back enough to meet my gaze, a nervous glint in her eyes. "Did you ever get disappointed? Like after you'd dragged it out for days, when you finally opened that last special present, it wasn't what you hoped for?"

I frame her face in my hands, thumbs brushing her lips. "Never. Waiting always made it better. Made me appreciate the gift more. Made me want to take care of it. Cherish it. Keep it forever."

Her lips part, but before she can say anything to remind me that she's thinking of this as a "holiday fling" that isn't going to last, I scoop her off the counter and carry her over to the quilts.

I lower her down, kissing her again. "Now," I whisper against her mouth, "let's start unwrapping."

CHAPTER 17
SHIRA
6 DAYS UNTIL I HAVE TO LEAVE

Finally.

Jonny lays me down on the nest of blankets he stole for us, gazing down at me like I'm the gift he's been waiting for. I reach for the hem of my new ugly sweater, but he stops me, holding my hand.

"Nope," he says, smirking. "That's my job."

Happy to comply, I settle back against the quilt he laid over the rug, which isn't nearly as soft and comfortable as it looks. But I'm not about to say anything that could put the brakes on this moment. Jonny reaches down and slowly lifts the sweater his sisters made for me, pausing when it's over my face.

"What?" I say, muffled from under my sweater.

"Just admiring the view." His voice is a little rough, like he's finding this slow restraint just as painful as I am.

"You should probably see it all, then." Smiling, I lift my arms so he can slip the sweater over my head.

Instead of tossing it to the side, he folds it and puts it beneath my head like a pillow. "That's better," he murmurs. His gaze drifts down my body, then back up to my face, his eyes

148

shining with a mixture of desire and something else. Tenderness, maybe? "You are just the prettiest thing."

My cheeks flush. "You think so?"

"From the very first time I saw you."

Slowly, he lowers himself over me, lips skimming lightly over my lips before dropping down to my neck. He nips at my collarbone, tasting as he makes his way down. "How do you taste like this?" he whispers.

"Like what?"

"Sweet. Like powdered sugar and vanilla."

I'm about to answer when he puts his hands on me—big and warm and a little rough, spanning my waist, sliding up to my ribs to my breasts until he's palming me, his thumbs brushing against my nipples. They stiffen against the lacy fabric of my bra, and I arch my back. A soft moan slips out of my mouth.

"That sound," he murmurs, his eyes drifting closed, his forehead knotting almost like he's in pain. "I need more of that."

But he doesn't move to take my bra off yet. He's lost in some private haze, lips tracing a slow, deliberate path from my neck to my collarbone to between my breasts, while his hands roam like they own every curve of me.

He hums, low, appreciative, as if everything he touches and tastes is delicious. I'm lit up like a menorah on the last night of Hanukkah, every nerve ending flickering with desire. When he puts his mouth right over my nipple and sucks through the fabric of my bra, a sharp bolt of heat runs through me. I moan again, louder.

"Yeah, like that," he says, his voice low. "Let me hear how I make you feel."

We're not even naked, and I think this might already be the best sex I've ever had.

Slowly, methodically, taking his time like I knew he would, he kisses his way down my belly, stopping at the waistband of my jeans.

He looks up at me; his eyes are almost primal in their intensity. "Yes?" he asks, his fingers on the button of my jeans.

"Yes," I say, my breath already growing erratic. "Yes to all of it, to everything. You can do whatever you want with me."

"Good news for me; bad news for you." His lips quirk in a smile as he unzips my jeans. I lift my hips so he can slide them down, taking his sweet time, peeling them off me before tossing them aside.

"You are so fucking beautiful," he says, looking down at me with something like awe on his face.

"Don't tell me," I say, wrapping my leg around his. "Show me."

"Yes, ma'am." He hooks his thumbs inside my panties and sends them off in the same direction as my jeans. Normally, I might move to cover myself, pull the blanket over me, but the way his eyes glaze over as they drift down my body, it's clear he likes what he sees. "Fuck, Shira, I want you so bad."

"Then hurry up and take me."

"Patience," he teases. "I'm getting there."

He crawls over me, still fully dressed—which I want to remedy, but first...his mouth claims mine in a deep, hungry kiss that leaves me breathless. He takes my bottom lip between his, sucking gently as his hand drifts down. I bend my knee and let my legs fall open, giving him full access. "That's right," he murmurs against my mouth, before kissing me again.

His fingers find my center, circling and stroking, like I showed him the other night. Heat pools in my stomach, sliding down my legs like liquid gold. The man pays attention, and there's nothing hotter than that.

"How do you feel this good?" he asks, his eyes drifting

closed as he dips a finger inside me, then another. "So ready for me."

I squirm beneath him, lifting my hips, urging him deeper as my breathing quickens. "Been ready for you for a while," I say, then gasp as he slides his fingers to a spot that makes me light up.

His breath is hot on my ear as he whispers, "I need to taste you."

"Do it."

He smirks and gives me one more kiss before his lips trail back down my body, settling between my legs. My hands grip the blanket beneath me, bracing myself for what's coming next. But of course, he still takes his time, slowly lifting my left leg so it's resting on his shoulder as he kisses down my thigh.

Then he presses his tongue flat against me, and my hips jump.

"Jonny," I gasp.

"Yes, love?"

"More of that."

His low chuckle rumbles through me as he tastes me, teasing, exploring. I reach down, sliding my hands into his hair, letting my nails rasp against his scalp. "Oh yeah," he groans. "More of *that.*"

And I'm happy to oblige, loving that I can make him feel good while he makes *me* just about lose my mind. He's still taking his time, circling, sucking, paying attention to every sound I make. Soon, I'm boneless, a bundle of nerves, sparking to life at his every touch.

I keep one hand in his hair but slip the other one under my bra, pinching my nipple to heighten the sensation. His tongue flicks against my center, and suddenly, I am starlight. My back arches, my legs tighten, and I cry out, riding the wave of ecstasy as he holds my hips in place and continues to draw out every last drop of pleasure from me.

When I open my eyes again, Jonny's next to me, propped up on an elbow, looking down at me with a satisfied smile.

"I am so pissed at you," I whisper, barely able to form the words.

His eyebrows pull together. "Why?"

"For making me wait so long for that."

He laughs and pulls me closer to him, pressing a kiss to the top of my head. "I'll have to make up for lost time while I've got you, then."

His words send a tiny pang through my chest, a reminder that we don't have many days left. But I tell myself to focus on what I've got right now, in front of me.

"I have a very serious question for you," I say.

"Yeah?"

"Why aren't you naked?"

His face breaks into a grin. "You're so horny it's adorable."

"I've been thinking about it since you fixed my shelves." I tug him down so he's on his back, then swing my leg so I'm straddling his hips. "I'm not normally like this."

"What are you normally like?"

"Reserved." I take off my bra, the last piece of clothing I have left, and watch his eyes grow wide. "Responsible. Really, really patient."

"Interesting," he says, reaching up to touch me, and the feeling of his hands on my skin, his fingers on my nipples, sends goosebumps running down my arms and legs. "Because with me you've been reckless, needy, desperate—"

I smack his chest lightly, and he catches my hand. "Irresistible," he says, pressing my hand to his lips. "Sexy. Gorgeous."

My hands move to the top button of his shirt, undoing it with trembling fingers. Jonny shifts beneath me, wincing.

I stop, mid-button. "Is this okay?"

"Yeah," he says. "Don't stop—the ground is just...concrete under this."

I laugh, and my fingers start moving again. "We could go back to your truck?"

"Nope. We're not moving. Get on with it."

"Yes, sir." I finally reach the last button and open his shirt. My hands falter. None of my previous experiences with men have prepared me for what I'm seeing now.

Of course, he'd have a body like this—broad, muscular shoulders and chest, the right side covered in black ink that crawls from his pec to his shoulder. When he sits up enough so he can shrug out of his shirt, I see that the tattoo curls down to his elbow. I'd love to trace every inch of it with my tongue, but I can't stop staring at the rest of him: sun-warmed skin, lean muscles, and a faint line of light-brown hair arrowing from his navel into his waistband.

"The farther this goes, the more pissed off at you I'm getting," I tell him, running my hands over his chest. "How dare you look this good and keep me waiting so long?"

He only grins in response, folding one hand back behind his head in a lazy, confident pose that makes my mouth go dry and my thighs tighten around him.

"You're impossible," I tell him, though I'm smiling.

"Yet you keep coming back for more."

Shaking my head, I scoot down on his body so I can unbutton his jeans.

"How mad am I going to be when I take off your pants?" I say, running my fingers, feather light, over the bulge in his jeans.

Jonny hisses in pleasure. "You'll forgive me the second I'm inside you."

He's probably right, based on the sneak peek I got in the truck. I unzip his jeans, eager to get a good look at him. Jonny lifts his hips, and I slide his jeans down.

A laugh bursts out of me when I see his boxers.

Jonny grins. "You like?"

"I like," I say, admiring the boxers that say, "Big Dreidel Energy" with a bunch of smiling dreidels dancing all around. "But they've got to go."

The boxers get added to the pile of our discarded clothes, and I wrap my fingers around him, stroking as I lick my lips. "Everything really is bigger in Texas," I tease, lowering my mouth to take him in.

"*Fuck,*" Jonny hisses as I swirl my tongue around his tip, bobbing my head to take him as deep as I can while I continue to stroke his length. He's leaning up on one arm, his other hand wrapped around my hair, holding it up so he can watch exactly what I'm doing.

"Shira." He says my name like it's a gift, like I'm a gift, and I reward him by taking him even deeper. His hips pulse, and I can tell he's holding himself back. "Yes, *yes*, just like that. So good. *So fucking good.*"

His words make me want to give him even more, so I drop my jaw and let him sink all the way back. He rewards me with a low groan that makes my entire body go hot. I pull back just before I start to gag—there is nothing sexy about that—and turn my attention back to his tip, swirling my tongue around him.

Suddenly, Jonny sits up. His eyes are wild, pupils blown out. "I need to be inside you. Now."

Before I can even respond, he pulls me toward him so I'm on

his lap, chest to chest, my knees straddling his hips. He dives in for a kiss, all tongue and teeth and desperate gasps. His hands are everywhere—gripping my waist, sliding over my back, fisting in my hair, claiming me completely. He's hard against my stomach, and I'm aching to reach down and guide him where I want him.

Before I lose myself completely, I pull back enough to lean over and grab my jeans to pull out the condom I tucked in my pocket earlier. It's wrapped in gold paper, with a bow tied around it.

"One more gift," I say, handing it to him.

His eyes lock on mine as he unties the bow with his teeth before tearing the package open. "Impressive."

"I've gotten really good at gift wrapping since working here."

"And unwrapping."

He hands me the condom, eyebrows raised, and I take it. He clenches his jaw and exhales sharply as I roll it on him. Then I lift up and position myself so he's at my entrance.

"Take your time," he says, voice low.

He's right to warn me because even though I'm dying to move quickly, he's bigger than I'm used to. Slowly, I lower myself, my eyelids fluttering at the intensity of the stretching.

"That's right," he whispers, like he's coaching me along. "So good. You take me so well."

He's watching me with a gaze so dark and intense it steals my breath. The tendons in his neck are standing out, like he's trying to restrain himself.

But we've waited too long to let this be anything less than everything.

"Don't hold back," I say.

"We'll get there." He lifts a hand to brush my hair away from my face, then slides his hand into my hair, cradling the back of my head. Slowly, carefully, watching my face, he rocks his hips.

I moan, my eyes fluttering closed.

"Eyes on me." His voice is low. Commanding.

I obey, opening my eyes to meet his—dark blue, flickering in the candlelight. Another slow roll of his hips, deeper now, and I whimper softly.

He pauses, eyes narrowed as he searches my face.

I take a shuddering breath, then nod. "More."

The corner of his mouth lifts in a dangerous smirk. "That's my girl."

He keeps one hand cradling my head and slides the other down to cup my ass, guiding me in a leisurely rhythm. He's murmuring words of appreciation, telling me I'm beautiful, that he's never felt anything so good in his life, that I'm everything he wants. My body flushes with pleasure; I've never been with a man who said things like this during sex. Knowing that I'm pleasing him, that he's enjoying this as much as I am, makes everything better.

He shifts his hips, and the next thrust hits something new inside me. Pleasure flares so sharply it's almost pain. My eyes roll back, and a helpless sound escapes my throat. "*Jonny...*"

"Look at me, love."

I force my eyes open, blinking through the haze. His face fills my vision—flushed, a lock of hair falling across his forehead. His eyes are fierce. Raw. Like he's barely holding it together.

"Shira." He thrusts into me again, harder. "Stay with me."

The words send a shockwave through me, a plea wrapped in a command. "I'm here."

His breath catches, his rhythm faltering. "Stay with me," he says again, but softer now, like a prayer.

"I'm not going anywhere." I grip his shoulders tighter, anchoring us both.

"Not tonight. Not ever."

Heat surges through me. He moves faster, desperation edging into every thrust, his hands gripping me as if I'm the only thing holding him together. "Stay," he growls, almost pleading now.

The word cracks something open in me, and I arch into him, gasping. He breaks, shuddering against me, arms locking around me like he never wants to let me go, holding me so tightly it aches.

And even though I know he doesn't mean *stay*, as in forever, in this moment, it feels possible. Here, in this candlelit bookshop, with his arms around me, his heart beating in sync with mine. A single, reckless thought flares in my mind—I don't want to leave this man.

CHAPTER 18

JONNY

5 DAYS UNTIL SHE'S GONE

When I was a kid, I used to wish I had a magic remote control for life. One that would let me fast-forward through math class, mute my parents when they lectured me about responsibility, and change the channel whenever the day got boring. As I grew up, I realized it wouldn't be worth it, because all those moments—painful, beautiful, or complicated —shape who we are.

But right now, I'd give anything for that remote. I'd hit pause, hold the frame exactly here: Saturday morning, waking up in Shira's bed for the first time.

She's curled against me, skin warm under the sheets, dark hair spilling across the pillow. Her breathing is slow and even, every exhale brushing against my skin like a secret. There's a softness to her in sleep that floors me. Last night she was all fire and teasing and hands in my hair; now she's a quiet miracle in the morning light. I trace her shoulder with my thumb, memorizing the slope of it, the tiny freckles I hadn't noticed before.

After what happened at the market last night, I knew there was no way I was leaving this woman to sleep in my childhood room alone, but I also wasn't interested in sleeping in the bookshop and being caught in the morning. So we dressed again, straightened ourselves up, and slipped out into the night.

When we reached her place, I got to unwrap her all over again, savoring it even more because I wasn't frantic and half-blinded by desire. Instead, I was awake to every sound she made, every breath against my neck, every inch of her skin under my hands.

But it isn't just her body that makes me lose my mind. It's the way she laughs in the middle of kissing, the way she asks questions that crack me open, the way she looks at me like she sees straight through the bullshit I've built up over the years.

Now all I want is to stay in this moment with the sheets tangled around us, her heart steady against mine. Stay here where it's simple. Where it's safe. Where she's warm and soft and *mine*.

I slide my palm down the smooth dip of her waist, to the swell of her hip. She sighs in her sleep and rolls closer, fitting herself against me. My heart lurches—an ache so sweet it almost hurts—and I bury my face in her hair, breathing her in.

"Mmmm." Her voice is drowsy as she nuzzles into my chest. "I could get used to this."

Me, too.

"How are you feeling this morning?" I murmur, brushing her hair back from her face. I'd happily let her sleep another couple of hours—God knows she deserves it after last night—but the market will be opening soon. It's the final stretch, the last weekend before the holiday.

She blinks up at me, bleary-eyed and so damn cute. "So good."

"Not too sore?"

Biting her lip, she hesitates, then shakes her head. "Not at all."

I lower my brows. "Liar."

She laughs, eyes shining. "Okay, yes, I'm sore—but in a good way. Reminds me of what you did to me."

"Just say the word, and I'll do it again."

"Now, please." She rolls to her back, stretching her arms and legs wide in a lazy sprawl. "I'm ready."

I can't help laughing as I roll on top of her, bracing myself on my forearms so I don't crush her. "You need to get ready for *work*."

Her eyes fly open. "Oh, shit—what time is it?"

"Nine thirty-five. The market opens at ten, right?"

She groans, draping an arm over her face. "Ugh. I need to shower. And wash my hair. I'm a total mess."

"A beautiful mess." I nudge her legs apart and settle between them. Leaning down, I brush my lips along her jaw. "I have an offer for you."

"Mmmm?"

"How about you take your time getting ready, and I'll open the shop."

She sighs, half protest, half surrender. "No, it's fine..."

"Let me take care of you," I murmur, kissing a slow path down her neck. "You went through a lot last night. You're probably pretty worn out."

She lets out a soft snort. "Such an ego."

"Ego?" I smirk. "How is it *my* ego when *you* were the one who kept saying things like, *Don't stop, more, please, yes...*"

"Pretty sure that was you, Mr. Dirty Talk. *Such a good girl, that's right baby, deeper, tighter, fuuuuuuck...*"

Laughing, I roll us over so she's on top of me now, her hair falling around her shoulders, framing us in a dark curtain. "You liked it."

"I did," she says, leaning down to kiss me. "A lot. So yes, I will accept your offer. You can open the shop for me so I can shower and take my time getting ready. On one condition."

I arch a brow. "Name it."

She fixes me with those big brown eyes, lips curving slow and wicked. "How about you make something up to me? Last night, you refused to fuck me against the wall. And...my shower has a wall."

I picture steam curling off her body, water beading on her skin. Heat licks down my spine.

"Shira..." I drag my thumb across her lower lip. "You're not gonna be able to walk straight after all this."

She grins. "Walking straight's overrated."

Forty minutes later—fifteen minutes after the bookstore should have opened, which frankly feels heroic given what transpired in Shira's bathroom—I'm whistling as I walk in the back door to the market. It's already buzzing with kids darting between booths, adults balancing cups of coffee and shopping bags, and Christmas music playing. I stop by the quilt and candle shops, slipping each of them some cash for the stuff I took last night, and keep moving.

When I reach the bookshop, there's a mini-mob waiting. A couple of them I recognize, but most are strangers to me. That makes me smile, thinking of people driving in from other towns. Coming here to shop at our market.

"Mornin', sorry about the delay," I say, as I cut through the crowd.

A man with a handlebar mustache frowns at me. "Where's Shira?"

"She'll be here in an hour or so," I tell him.

"Well, she's supposed to help me pick out gifts for my daughters," he says, sounding panicked.

"She ordered a cookbook for my mother-in-law," Mrs.

Hinshaw chimes in, following me with the crowd as I make my way over to the register.

"She should have some books on hold for me," a man I don't know says.

"She promised me we'd talk about the ending to *The Silent Patient* when I finished it," Mrs. Landry says, holding the book aloft.

They're all clamoring at once, and even though it's over-whelming, I love it. Seeing her through their eyes, this smart, thoughtful, caring woman who knows exactly how to connect with each individual. They clearly adore her, and I get it. I feel the same way.

There it is again, that twinge in my chest, pride and longing and something scarier I'm not ready to name.

"All right, hold your horses," I say, raising a hand. "One at a time."

When Shira arrives an hour later, I've dealt with most of the customers who were waiting, and the bookshop is calmer, with just a few people browsing. When she comes around the corner and spots me at the register wearing her red apron, her face breaks into a smile. I find myself smiling back, goofy and wide and not at all cool.

But God, I love looking at her. All that glossy dark hair cascading over her shoulders, those full lips, that sweater that hugs her curves just right. I especially love that I got to see her come undone last night and again this morning.

And now a greedy, possessive part of me whispers that I don't want anyone else to see her like that. Ever.

Mine.

Blinking that away, I smile as she walks up. She's carrying a cupholder with two coffees and a bag from the bakery a few doors down.

"There you go, sir," she says, setting them down on the counter. "Payment for your...assistance this morning."

She grins at me, eyes twinkling like she's thinking back to what we were doing earlier—her back against the tile wall, her legs around my waist. But there's a touch of awkwardness in the way she stands, shoulders a little tighter, gaze flicking to mine and away again. As though she's not quite sure how this is supposed to go after the line we finally crossed.

I come around the counter, wrap my arms around her waist, and press a soft kiss to her lips. "I missed you."

"It's been like an hour," she says, smiling up at me.

"Way too long." I untie the apron and lift it over my head, then put it over hers. "Much cuter on you."

I give her one more kiss, then step back before we get complaints for ruining the family-friendly atmosphere. "Your customers are nuts, by the way. Totally unhinged. But I did my best to help the ones I could. Took notes on the ones I couldn't."

"Oh?"

She leans in as I show her the notepad where I've been jotting things down.

"Mr. Martinez still needs recs for his daughters, but he gave me a few ideas to pass on to you. Mrs. Frandsen says she'll swing by later today for the computer book you're ordering for her?"

"*Coding for Dummies*," she says, nodding. "It came in yesterday—I'll call her."

"Lindy Turner came in. Skipping Saturday morning chores to come to the bookshop, apparently. Kids these days." I sigh and shake my head, mock-disappointed. "Anyway, she said you have a book for her, but she wanted to make sure it's in a paper sack or something? No idea why."

"It's a romance between two girls who meet at summer camp," she says. "She's nervous about anyone seeing it."

I nod, taking that in. "Beth Thompson stopped by, too. Apparently, her grandma was Jewish, and she's wondering if you have any books about Jewish holidays? She wants to get one for herself and for her dad."

Shira lights up. "Sure, I can find some."

I continue down the list, and she listens, making notes and nodding as if she's got all this under control.

"You're incredible at this," I say, when I finish.

She looks up, surprised. "I'm just selling books."

"No, it's much more than that. They trust you. They trust your recommendations. You know these people. They love you, Shira."

"I don't know about that," she says, shaking her head. "But I have enjoyed it more than I expected."

She moves around to the register, straightening things up, getting settled in for the morning. A customer walks in, and Shira greets him by name, asking if he needs help finding anything. I lean against the counter, sip my coffee, and watch her.

It's not just that she's good at this, though she is. It's that she's brought something different to this town. This shop has, too. New perspectives, fresh ideas, a spark that feels almost contagious. She's not just running a bookshop—she's creating something vibrant, inclusive, and unique. I think of the book she gave me a few days ago, *East of Eden*, and how she picked it for me. I realize recommending a book is more than sharing a story—it's a way of seeing someone, noticing who they are, and inviting them to explore something they might never have discovered on their own.

Turning, I scan the rest of the market, the other shops and booths tucked against the brick walls, people milling about.

Next year, this won't exist. I find myself wishing for that magic remote again, desperate to pause this scene, too. Hold onto it all a little longer.

"How's the coffee?" Shira says, and I snap back to attention, realizing she's done helping that customer.

"Oh. It's great. I should run home and change. My parents are probably wondering what happened to me last night."

She raises an eyebrow. "Are they going to be scandalized? Think I'm a terrible influence on their son?"

"Nah," I say with a smirk, "they're probably hoping I haven't been a terrible influence on *you*."

"Well, you have," she says, grinning. "You've got me thinking about all kinds of things I shouldn't be thinking about..."

I lean in, brushing my lips against her ear. "Then do me a favor—keep thinking them. All day long. Let 'em simmer. I'll taste the proof tonight."

Her eyes flare with heat. "Deal."

I sneak another quick kiss, then hesitate, a knot forming in my stomach. "You're still leaving the morning of the twenty-fifth?"

Her smile fades, just slightly. "Yeah. Why?"

Because it's way too soon, and I'm freaking out.

"Just...checking. I didn't know if your plans had changed."

She hesitates. "Why would my plans change?"

"I don't know. No reason." I glance away, running a hand through my hair.

When I look back at her, her face has softened. She tilts her head, lips parting like she's not sure how to respond. "Jonny...."

"No, I get it," I blurt, before she has to figure out how to let me down easy. "You've got plans with your friends, and you've got that big promotion to bag, right?"

She nods slowly, eyes fixed on me. "Right."

"Right," I repeat, like a moron.

Last night was earth-shattering for me—I mean, I practically begged her to stay with me—but apparently it didn't have that big of an impact on her. Not enough to consider staying longer, anyway. Which, yeah, good to know. I need to keep my expectations in check. Just because I'm drowning in all these warm and gushy feelings doesn't mean she is. Just because my throat is tightening with the urge to blurt the words *don't go* doesn't mean she wants to hear them.

What would I even say, anyway? *Stay and hang out with me longer because I might be dangerously addicted to you?* She has ambitions. Goals. That's part of why I like her so damn much. Even if she did postpone her return by a few days, it would only prolong the inevitable. Eventually, she has to return to her real life. And once my family doesn't need me here anymore, I need to figure out my next steps.

A new image rushes into my mind: walking down the streets of Chicago with her, both of us bundled up in hats, scarves, and gloves, her arm hooked around mine. The icy wind off the lake is whipping her hair around her, her cheeks and nose red from the cold, as I pull her toward me and kiss her forehead...

Get it together, I order myself. I must be losing my fucking mind. Maybe it's because I took things slow physically—it scrambled me up, and now my feelings are sprinting way ahead. It's been less than a month since we met. It's been less than a *day* since we slept together. For her, this thing between us has probably just been a pleasant interlude, a way to make her time here a little more tolerable. A *holiday hookup.*

We're just having fun, I remind myself. And that's great. It *is.*

"Jonny?" she says, bringing me back to reality.

I clear my throat and take a step back. "I'll see you soon, okay?"

Her eyes dim. "Sure. Yeah. See you soon."

Once I get out to the parking lot and sink into my dad's truck, the tightness in my chest doesn't ease. If anything, it gets worse, like my ribs are too small for my heart. In a few days, *all* of this will be gone. Shira. The bookshop, the holiday, this version of me that exists when I'm with her...it'll vanish like breath in winter air.

A new thought rises—wild, stupid, completely irrational. If I can't keep her, maybe I can keep *something*. A fragment of this perfectly magical holiday season that won't disappear when she does.

Instead of turning left on Main to head toward home, I turn right. The truck rumbles down streets I've driven my whole life, under the old Christmas garland strung across Main Street and the tinselly decorations clinging to the lampposts. Exactly the same as when I lived here as a kid.

But then I pass the town square, where the giant Christmas tree sits opposite the towering menorah I built for her. A reminder that things *can* change here. Traditions can expand. New perspectives can be heard.

For so long, this place felt like gravity, like if I stayed too long, I'd be pulled under and stuck here. But this year, staying for the whole holiday season instead of just popping in for Thanksgiving and Christmas before hurrying off, I've been forced to slow down. To spend real time with my family again, feeling the chaos and the love. Most of all, meeting Shira, getting to know her, seeing the way she moves through the world—it's made me think differently. Like maybe you don't have to hide pieces of yourself to belong. Maybe you can still be fully you and also part of something bigger. Maybe *I* can.

And maybe I can leave my own mark on this town. Make a positive difference for the future.

After a couple of blocks, I pull up in front of an unassuming brick building, gripping the steering wheel as I stare at the first-floor window. The words *Kensington Realty* are stenciled across it.

I went to school with Michael Kensington. He was everything I wasn't: responsible, respectful, hard-working. Still is, from what my parents say.

Heart pounding, I get out of the truck and walk into the office.

A woman with short dark hair looks up from the front desk.

"Hey there," I say, recognizing her; she was a couple of years behind me in school. "Emily Wilson, right?"

She smiles. "Emily Kensington now."

"Oh, you and Mike are..."

"Married for three years," she says, holding up her left hand to show the ring. "What brings you in, Jonny? Can I help you with something?"

"Uh, yeah." I stuff my hands in my pockets and rock back on my heels. "Is Mike available? I don't have an appointment or anything, just wanted to ask him a quick question."

"Sure, let me grab him."

She steps around through the door behind the desk, and soon Mike comes out—a little heavier, a lot balder, but clearly happy and successful-looking.

"Jonny McKay, good to see you," he says, coming over and shaking my hand. "What can I do for you?"

I shift my weight, looking down at the floor for a second before glancing back up. "I was wondering if you could look into a property for me."

He folds his arms, nodding. "Sure. What's the property?"

"You know the old textile mill, where the holiday market's happening this year?" I pause. "I'd like to buy it."

CHAPTER 19

SHIRA

The market is usually closed on Sundays, but since Christmas is just around the corner, it's opening today at noon. For most of the town of Azalea, that translates to "after church," but for Jonny and me, it means after a brunch date.

We're at Minnie's, a local diner that's surprisingly packed. Jonny's sitting across from me in the booth, his back straight and shoulders squared. It's not the body language of a man who is apologetic for taking up space in this town, who is constantly aware of the way people see and judge him.

"Earth to Shira," Jonny says, nudging his foot against mine. "Where'd you drift off to?"

"I'm here," I say. "Just thinking."

"About…"

"So nosy," I tease. "If you must know, I was thinking about you."

"Exactly which part of me are you thinking about?" he says with a sly grin.

"My favorite part."

His eyebrows shoot up. "My smile? I bet it's my radiant smile."

Laughing, I roll my eyes. "Close. It does have something to do with your mouth."

"Which part of my mouth, exactly?" He leans in, voice dropping low. "Lips? Tongue? Teeth?"

I put a hand to my chest, gasping like I'm scandalized. "Excuse me, sir! I meant having a *conversation* with you."

He lets out a dark laugh. "Right."

"And everything else that mouth can do," I add in a whisper, grinning.

He grins back, eyebrows dancing as he cuts into his giant stack of blueberry pancakes. "So, are you sad that Hanukkah is going to be over after tonight?"

"Not at all," I say without hesitation.

Jonny looks surprised. "If I could get seven days and eight nights of Christmas..." He pauses to think. "I'd probably be exhausted."

I laugh. "The first few days are always exciting, but the novelty usually wears off by night six. And then it starts to feel repetitive, which it is." I hesitate, not sure how to explain the deeper significance and weight of the holiday, how the "fun" and excitement are just a tiny part of it.

"But..."

I smile, grateful for Jonny's genuine curiosity and desire to learn; it's been such a wonderful gift. All the orgasms aside, I've really appreciated how open he's been to letting me share something that means so much to me.

And this isn't stuff I talk about. But with him, I feel okay to share, even if it reveals a side of me that's a little dark and morbid.

"But when I start to get that 'ugh, again,' feeling, I try to remind myself of everything my ancestors went through, what they lived and died for, and I realize it's an honor and a privilege to be able to celebrate our holidays openly, and I shouldn't take that freedom for granted."

I think back to when I first arrived in Azalea, and how my instinct was to hide that part of myself. If I'd kept it hidden, a secret, I would have missed out on so much connection with this incredible community.

"But the last night, that goes back to being exciting and fun, right?" he says.

"It does," I admit. "It's kind of like the climax. And with every candle lit, the menorah is at its brightest, like the light and the miracle are at completion. Plus, when I was a kid, that was the night I'd usually get the biggest gift."

"Ahhh," Jonny says. "So, I should get you a big gift for tonight?"

"No," I say, shaking my head for emphasis. "You already gave me the only gift I wanted—at the market, in bed, in the shower...and it was a *big* gift."

"Tsk, tsk, tsk," Jonny says, mock-serious as he reaches under the table and squeezes my knee. "I wonder if all your bookstore fans know what a dirty mind you have?"

"Who, me?" I tease, playfully batting my eyes as I calculate how many hours I have to wait to jump his bones again.

We take our time finishing our breakfast, neither of us in a rush to go our separate ways.

"Tell me about Christmas Eve at the McKay house," I ask, hoping, but not assuming, that I'll be invited to experience it myself.

Jonny leans back in the booth, a fond smile on his face, the evidence of many happy memories. "There's always a big feast —usually tamales. And then, there's a tractor parade down Main Street."

I burst out laughing. "Seriously?"

"Dead serious. Everyone decorates their tractors with tinsel and lights, and then we drive 'em down the center of town. Lots of people ride their horses, too. It's super country." He grins, then nudges my foot with his boot. "How about you? Tell me how Shira Schwartz celebrates Christmas Eve."

"Well, the last few years, my friends and I have gone to the Matzo Ball."

"Like the soup?"

"No, like a ball. A dance. We get all dressed up, there's a DJ, and usually an open bar."

"All the ranch waters you can drink," Jonny teases.

"I'm usually more of a vodka soda girl," I tell him, and it strikes me just how much I've changed since coming down here. For the first time, I'm worried if I'll still fit in back home with my friends, the one place I've always felt like I belonged.

"I'm sorry you're missing it," Jonny says.

"It's okay—I'll be home in time for the best part."

"Right. Your Chinese food and a movie tradition." He's focused on his pancakes again, his expression unreadable as he takes another bite.

With the exception of the other night, Jonny hasn't flat-out asked me to stay—and things said in the middle of mind-blowing sex don't count. Besides, he could have just been asking me to stay there with him that night. In that moment, on the edge of an orgasm that had been weeks in the making, I wasn't about to stop and ask him to clarify.

And as amazing as this month away has been, I know this isn't real life—for either one of us. This was always meant to be temporary. I have a job to get back to, and most importantly, my friends. As much as we've tried to stay connected while I've been here, it isn't the same.

Our group chat has been pretty quiet lately, and I can't help the nagging voice in my head, reminding me that this is exactly how it started with Anya. It wasn't anyone's intention or fault, just a slow, quiet drifting apart. I don't want that to happen with me—another reason I need to get back home where I belong.

I look up from my plate to Jonny, who's watching me.

"We should probably get going," he says, clearing his throat. "We don't want another angry mob at the store."

He raises his hand, signaling for the check.

I reach for my purse. "Let me get this one."

"Absolutely not," Jonny says, putting his wallet on the table. "Millionaire, remember."

I playfully roll my eyes. "Fine, then thank you." He pulls a hundred-dollar bill out of his wallet and sets it on the table.

"You know, I still wanted to bang you back when I thought you were the broke handyman."

Jonny laughs. "Thank you?"

"I'm just saying, your money is the least interesting thing about you. And I want you to know that's not why I'm here with you."

"Why are you here with me?" His expression turns serious, and I get the feeling we're not playing around anymore. But even though I've been flirting with the idea of trying to find a way to make this work after my time here is up, I'm not ready for such a serious conversation.

Rather, I'm not ready for how this specific serious conversation might go. As far as I know, the last few weeks have just been a game for Jonny. Something to keep him entertained while he's stuck in town. And if that's the case, I don't want to know.

"Well," I say, "I'm here because you make me laugh. You make me think. And you make me come like no other."

Jonny laughs, a single note that's void of any humor. My face falls, and I hate myself a little for turning this into a joke.

Especially when the first two things are so true and mean so much.

We walk out of the diner, quiet and lost in our own thoughts, when I hear someone call my name.

I turn to see Miguel, who has become one of my best customers, purchasing bilingual books as fast as I can get them in stock.

"Hi, Miguel," I say, hugging him. "So good to see you—are you going to breakfast?" I nod toward the diner.

"No, mija, our restaurant is next door." He nods over toward the taqueria where I ordered my Thanksgiving dinner. The night I first met Jonny.

"Morning, Miguel," Jonny calls. "I've got to get our girl to the bookstore. Give Rosa my love."

Miguel tips an imaginary hat toward Jonny and gives me a wave before heading into the taqueria.

Once we're in the truck and Jonny is backing out of the parking lot, I say, "All these weeks, I had no idea Miguel was connected to the taqueria."

"He's been in the bookshop?" Jonny asks.

"Oh yeah," I tell him. "A few times, getting books in English and Spanish for his grandkids."

Jonny steals a glance at me, his eyebrow arched in curiosity. "Rosa and Miguel don't have any kids. No grandkids, either."

"Huh," I say, thinking back to our exchanges. "He bought all these books for early readers, and—oh."

The truth hits me like a slap in the face, and I curse myself for making assumptions. Through all our conversations, I never once thought the books might be for Miguel himself.

"I didn't even consider—he speaks English so well."

Jonny nods. "Learning how to speak a language is a whole different thing than learning to read it. My Granddad McKay didn't read past about a third-grade level. Miguel was actually his right-hand man on the farm when I was growing up."

"But...he runs the restaurant?"

"Now, he does," Jonny says. "He and Rosa opened the taqueria about ten years back. But they're still like part of our family."

"That's why you were there on Thanksgiving," I say, "bringing them a plate."

"Yup," Jonny says. "It's a family tradition. Every year, Mom invites them to join us, and every year they thank her, but say somebody's got to stay open for people who don't have anywhere to go. Like a pretty bookseller who stumbled into town."

"Huh," I say again. I'm still wrapping my head around the whole thing when Jonny pulls up in front of the market. He puts the car in park, then wraps his arm around my waist and slides me toward him on the bench seat.

"Hi," he says.

"Hi," I say back, bringing my hand to cup his face, running my thumb across the rough stubble.

His lips find mine, and what starts as a sweet "see you later" quickly deepens into the kind of kiss that's a prelude to something more.

"How rude," I say, coming up for air. He gives me one of his sultry looks that instantly makes my panties damp, and I go in for another kiss. What am I thinking, even considering walking away from this man?

I'm about to swing my legs around his waist when a car honks, reminding me that it's daylight and his windows are not tinted.

I groan, reluctantly peeling myself away.

"Have a good day, love," Jonny says.

That final word is still echoing in my mind as I walk into the bookstore. He started out calling me darlin', with that country-boy swagger and wink, like he was playing a part. Fun, flirty, easy to brush off. But *love*...

I shake my head. He doesn't mean it like that, of course. In fact, he probably says it to every woman he sleeps with. It will do me good to remember that this was never meant to be something serious. It was always supposed to be a fun challenge and a way to make the time go by faster—an opportunity to try on a different side of myself.

For all I know, it was the same for him. A fun distraction with the one woman in Azalea who didn't know the Jonny McKay he used to be. I can't forget that.

Six hours later, my feet hurt, my back aches, and my heart is heavy. And not just because of Jonny and these confusing feelings I'm having for him. All day, I couldn't stop thinking about Miguel and so many other people I've gotten the chance to know at the bookshop. The teenagers who came in asking for books featuring kids who look like them or share some aspect of their identity. The group of older ladies who started purchasing and reading a new book each week to discuss together. The countless people who came in to buy books for Christmas gifts and just for themselves.

To me, books have always been a source of entertainment or escape. Sure, I would sometimes read a book or a memoir to learn about a new experience, but I never really thought about how a book could actually open up someone's world.

Jonny was trying to tell me as much the other night when he talked about how much having a bookstore has meant to this community. The reason it was so important to him that the market have one this year. He knew it wasn't just a place to buy books, and I can't believe it took me so long to see it myself.

Suddenly, the saddest thing about my leaving Azalea isn't what I'm personally going to lose, but what this town and all its new readers will suddenly be without.

"You're a million miles away," Jonny says as I climb into his truck after closing.

I shrug, feeling my eyes start to water. "It's just starting to hit me, how much I'm going to miss this place."

He pauses. "You know, you don't have to—"

My phone rings with a FaceTime call.

Jonny and I both look to see Maya's face lighting up my phone screen.

"Go ahead," he says, shifting the truck into drive.

I glance between him and the phone, knowing the girls are probably together, calling to wish me a happy last night of Hanukkah before they light the candles, eat latkes, and open gifts.

"I don't mind," Jonny says, so I tap to answer the call before it drops off.

"Happy Hanukkah!" The chorus of my best friends' voices brings tears to my eyes. As much as I've loved being here in Azalea with Jonny, I really have missed them.

"Where are you?" Maya asks.

"OMG, are you with your Texas hottie?" Naomi chimes in.

"Let us say hi," Talia begs.

I glance over at Jonny, who seems game and more than a little pleased at the nickname. I shift the camera so they can see us, and the two of us can see all three of them.

"Happy Hanukkah, y'all," Jonny says, dialing up the Texas drawl.

Naomi gasps. "You didn't tell us he had an accent."

"Such a panty dropper," Talia says, fanning herself.

"Guys," I warn, but they're having too much fun with this.

"Now I understand why we've barely heard from you this week," Maya says.

"At least she finally got some," Naomi says.

"Seriously," Talia agrees. "But dude, you should not have made our girl wait so long. You practically gave her blue balls!"

"Seriously," Maya agrees. "A vibrator can only get a girl by for so long."

My cheeks flush. I might have held a few details back if I'd had the foresight to expect this awkward conversation.

"It's okay," Naomi says. "It sounds like he was worth the wait."

"Never underestimate the power of a little Vitamin D," Maya adds.

"Or a *big* one," Talia quips.

The girls cackle, cracking themselves up.

"Okay," I say, bringing the camera back toward me. "I'll see you guys in a few days—and don't forget, we're having a double header this year."

There's a chorus of "Can't wait!" "Love you!" and "Miss you!" before I hang up.

"Please don't judge me by my friends," I say.

"Never," Jonny says, giving me a quick kiss. "I mean, you didn't judge me by my family."

I laugh. "But your family is sweet and nice, like you."

"And your friends are charming and funny, like you."

We get out of the truck, and he follows behind me as I unlock the door to the cottage.

"Do you think your friends are right?" he says quietly. "Was I an idiot to make us wait so long? We could have had so much more time."

I turn to face him; his expression is almost wistful. Suddenly, I want him to know that I don't regret a single thing about our time together.

"But the anticipation," I remind him. "That made it better, right?"

He gives a soft smile. "With you, there's only better."

"That doesn't make sense," I say, kissing him. "But there's only better with you, too."

After we eat dinner, Jonny does the dishes while I put the candles in the menorah. He stands beside me, his arm wrapped around my waist as I strike the match.

I inhale the smell of sulfur as the flame bursts to life. I hold it to the shamash and take a moment to appreciate the magnitude of this miracle and how much sharing the holiday with Jonny has meant to me before I light the candles and say the prayer.

"Happy Hanukkah, Shira," Jonny says, and I'm filled with a sturdy warmth, but also a sadness, knowing that if I'd just been honest earlier, I could have had him here with me every night. Then there would have been no reason for me to cry or to lie.

"Happy Hanukkah, Jonny," I say, turning so we're face to face.

He tucks a strand of hair behind my ear. "Thanks for letting me in to experience all this with you."

"Thank you for wanting to experience it with me." I slip my arms around his neck and look at him, this man who is so much more than I ever expected or even knew I wanted.

"Come here," I say, pulling him down to my level. His eyes flutter shut, and I kiss his eyelids, grateful for the way he managed to change the way I see so many things, including myself. I kiss the dimples on his cheeks, first the left, then the right, appreciating the way he's made me smile and laugh until my sides ache.

I turn my attention to his ears, gently nibbling on his lobes.

The way this man listens and actually hears me, not just what I'm saying but *why* I'm saying it. He's really unlike anyone I've ever met.

And finally, I press my lips to his—the source of so much conversation, and so much pleasure. I deepen the kiss, hoping we can pick up where we left off this morning when he so rudely got me all worked up before work.

"Wait," Jonny says. "I have something for you first."

"Uh oh," I say. "I told you no gifts."

"Okay." He goes in for another kiss. "I can return it."

"Don't you dare," I say, pulling back so he can run out to his truck.

Jonny lets himself back in a moment later, holding a gift the size of a Kleenex box, wrapped with blue paper and a white bow.

"Happy last night of Hanukkah, Shira," he says.

I sigh and take the box, unwrapping it slowly, the way it deserves to be opened. I untie the bow, then wrap the ribbon around my wrist like a corsage. The paper goes next, one corner at a time, revealing a plain, white box.

Jonny looks excited, almost impatient for me to open it, so I don't hesitate before popping the lid open.

I suck in a breath, staring. If the town menorah was the most extravagant gift I've ever received, this is the most beautiful.

"It's a snow globe," he says as I lift it from the box. "Custom-made."

"It's incredible," I say, bringing it up to eye level. The scene inside is an artistic representation of one I'd recognize anywhere. A couple is standing in the center who look remarkably like us—he's wearing jeans, boots, and a jacket that looks like a Carhartt, and she's got wavy brown hair, wearing jeans, a sweater, and even a tiny gold Jewish star around her neck.

They're—*we're*—embracing in front of a small shop that says "The Book Nook" on the front.

Inside the store, I can see not only books, but a Christmas tree and a menorah. And when I turn the snow globe upside down, little snowflakes rain down, just like they did on the night of the Christmas tree lighting.

"We can't pause time," Jonny says, "but I wanted to find a way to freeze these few weeks we've had together."

My vision blurs, and I wipe the tears from my eyes, looking up from this perfect gift to the thoughtful man who gave it to me. "I'd say you shouldn't have, but I am so glad you did."

And with that, I launch myself into his arms and start kissing his face, saying, "Now take me back to my room so you can unwrap *your* gift, Jonny McKay."

CHAPTER 20

JONNY

JUST ONE MORE DAY WITH HER

Somehow I blinked, and it's Christmas Eve.

Shira's been running herself ragged these past few days, so I've been at the bookshop as much as possible, trying to make sure she's not working herself into the ground. She keeps thanking me, but my motivations are selfish. I get to spend more time with her, and she has more energy left for things I want to do with her after hours, in and out of the bedroom.

We've crammed as much as possible into these last few days—shopping for my nieces and nephews, driving to nearby towns to check out new restaurants, catching a screening of *It's a Wonderful Life* at the tiny old Azalea theater. Everywhere we go, I hold her hand, try to memorize her laugh, the way she bites her lip when she's thinking, the pink in her cheeks when she notices me staring. All the details I'll need later, when she's gone.

Yet no matter how much I've tried to slow down time, here we are. The holiday market closes at noon today. And tomorrow, Shira will be gone.

I keep reminding myself to be grateful for what we've had.

She's clearly excited to get home, buzzing about seeing her friends, all the places she wants to eat in Chicago, and getting back to her job. And I'm genuinely happy for her. I *am*.

Even if it feels like someone's slowly carving a hole in my chest with a rusty knife.

When I walk into the market at a quarter past noon, half the shops are already stripped bare, crates stacked behind tables, twinkle lights unplugged and sagging. Vendors in Santa hats and flannel are wrapping breakables in tissue paper, counting cash boxes, and hollering "Merry Christmas!" Everyone looks tired, but they've got that satisfied glow you get after a hard push that paid off.

Over and over, I get stopped, folks thanking me for keeping the market going while Dad's recovering, for making it feel bigger and brighter this year. Mrs. Kendrick presses a jar of pecan pralines into my hands and tells me not to forget where I came from. Mr. Walters shakes my hand so hard it rattles my teeth.

I haven't told anyone yet that I'm under contract to purchase the building. My idea's still more dream than plan, and for now it feels good to keep it tucked close, a secret seed I can plant later when I figure out what it's supposed to grow into.

When I approach the bookshop and spot her, I'm hit with the wordless sensation of "*Oh, there you are*" that's started happening the past few days. Like familiarity and relief wrapped up in yearning. But right on its heels comes the gut-punch. Tomorrow she's leaving.

Shaking that off, I walk into the shop to where Shira's talking with four teenage boys wearing work boots and hoodies.

She glances up at me. "Jonny, they're telling me you asked them to meet you here?"

"That's right," I say, smiling at the boys. "Shira, these are a few of my cousins: Davey, Mason, Ben, and Cade. Boys, this is Miss Shira Schwartz."

Each of them politely says "nice to meet you, ma'am" while shaking her hand in turn. Grandma McKay would be proud.

"They're here to take down the shop," I explain to Shira.

"Jonny's paying us two hundred bucks each," Davey adds, grinning.

Shira whirls toward me, eyes wide. "Wait—what? I was planning on taking it all down this afternoon."

"Nope, not happening. Can't have my girl wasting our last day together doing manual labor."

Oops. Didn't mean to slip *my girl* in there.

Hoping she didn't notice, I press on. "Just tell the boys how you want everything packed, and they'll get it done perfectly. And if they don't..." I eye my cousins, eyebrows raised, "...then they won't get paid a penny."

The boys all straighten up, practically saluting me.

Meanwhile, Shira's eyes have gone all shiny. "Thank you."

"My pleasure." Pretty sure there's nothing in this world I like more than making things easier for her.

After giving detailed instructions to the boys, Shira gathers up a few things to take back to her place—her purse, a tote bag of books she's bringing home to Chicago, and a little roller bag filled with odds and ends.

I swoop in and take them from her, one by one. She puts a hand on her hip, looking up at me. "I need to carry *something*!"

I shift the tote to my other shoulder, then hold out my empty hand. "Here. You can carry that."

She laces her fingers through mine, shaking her head, even though there's a pleased flush creeping over her cheeks. "I can't open doors for myself, I can't pack up my own shop, I can't carry my own stuff—"

"Why should you?" I wink. "You've got me."

At least, for the next approximately eighteen hours.

Before we leave, Shira turns back, her eyes sweeping over the space one last time. The boys are already hustling—stacking unsold books, taking down shelves, racing through it all for their two hundred bucks. In a few hours, this space, which meant so much to so many people, will be empty, stripped down to its bare bones.

"Goodbye, little bookshop," Shira whispers, more to herself than to me. "Thanks for everything."

As we head out to the truck, the sun is shining, and the air is crisp and cool. Shira slides under my arm like it's the most natural thing in the world. *Mine.* The word hums under my skin, taunting me.

"I have to admit," she says, "when you introduced me to your cousins, my first thought was, 'Oh dear, there are *more* of you?'"

A laugh bursts out. "You've barely scratched the surface on all the McKays in this town. We descend on each other for a huge extended-family dinner on Christmas night—you definitely dodged a bullet, leaving before that."

There's a pause. "Yeah. Guess so."

We reach the truck, and I open her door for her, offering her my arm to help her climb in. When I come around to my side and get in, she's already sitting in the middle, right where I like her.

"What's the plan for this afternoon?" she asks, looking excited.

"Whatever you want. I thought we'd drive into Dallas, grab a late lunch, maybe catch a movie—"

"What? Why?" Her brow furrows.

"Because you deserve a break from Christmas," I tell her. "And then tonight, there's a Matzo Ball hosted by the JCC in Dallas. Apparently, it's a huge event. I mean, I know you won't know anyone there, but I thought it sounded fun? If you're not into that, I'm sure we could find a bar open somewhere, get you more of those ranch waters you love."

"Oh." The sound is a soft puff of air. "Okay. Cool."

She's quiet as I start up the truck and head out of the parking lot and onto the main road. It's not until we stop at a red light a few blocks away that she speaks again.

"If I weren't here, what would you be doing this afternoon?"

The honest answer—*nursing a beer and missing you*—flashes through me. That's not what she means.

"Usually, I get into town on Christmas Eve," I say. "So I mostly spend the day helping Mom and Dad with the last of the prep, making food for tonight and tomorrow, wrapping gifts, that kind of thing. After that, it'd be the stuff I told you about the other day—tamales, tractor parade—"

"Let's do that," she blurts.

I glance over. "Don't worry about me missing my family traditions. I've spent more time with them this month than the entire past decade. And I'll spend all day with them tomorrow. Today, I want to be with you. Doing what *you* want."

She gazes up at me, her eyes big and brown and serious. "I want to experience your holiday with you, Jonny. As much as I'm here for."

My heart basically turns to liquid. "Okay. I'd love that."

When we walk into the kitchen at my parents' house, it looks like the refrigerator exploded. Mom and Bianca are elbow-deep in food prep, with Maggie standing on a chair "helping." Shira steps in without hesitation, putting on one of Mom's old floral aprons and rolling up her sleeves. She measures flour into Mom's ancient Bosch mixer for the cinnamon roll dough, while I dice onions and peppers for the quiche. Then, we both help distract the twins when they start fighting over whose turn it is to stir. Shira's asking my mom about recipes, laughing at Bianca's jokes, "accidentally" dropping bits of cheese for the dogs. And every time I glance at her, it feels like my heart's being kneaded along with the dough.

When that's done, I take Shira home so she can clean up (joining her in the shower for a little quickie, naturally). Then we return to my parents' house for dinner. Isaac and Annabel picked up several dozen tamales from Rosa and Miguel's earlier today, and now the dining table is piled high with tamales, refried beans, rice, guacamole, and more. Shira slides into the chair next to mine as if it's always been her spot, unwrapping a tamale and joining the conversation without missing a beat. I try to eat, but I don't seem to have much of an appetite. Mostly, I'm just trying not to think about how next year she won't be here.

"Who's ready for the tractor parade?" Isaac says when we've all cleaned up dinner.

The little kids all cheer, "Meeeeee!"

"Let's get a move on then," Isaac says, turning to me and Shira. "Y'all want to join?"

I look at her, my eyebrows raised. "Up to you."

"Let's go," Shira says, smiling. "When am I going to get another chance to be in a tractor parade?"

Never. And shit, there's a lump in my throat.

"Great," I say, forcing a smile.

We all say bye to Dad, Kara, and Kyle—they're staying home, watching *A Christmas Story,* and eating cookies—then everyone heads outside. Earlier, Isaac and Bianca, along with their families, decked out the tractors with Christmas lights and tinsel. White string lights and green garland perfectly accent the fancy new Case IH Magnum's shiny red paint, and Granddad's old green and yellow John Deere is decorated with multicolored lights, with a set of "reindeer" antlers and a red rubber nose on the front.

Isaac takes charge, directing everyone to their designated locations. He'll drive the Magnum with Annabel and baby Nellie in the cab, and Jake and Emma will sit with Mom and Bianca's family in the small trailer hitched up to it. Everyone climbs into their places, and Sampson and Delilah jump in the trailer, tails wagging, matching red plaid bandanas around their necks.

"You want to take the Deere?" my brother asks me.

I blink, surprised. That's usually Dad's job. "Uh, sure."

Bianca hands me a Santa hat to put on, then Shira and I climb into the small cab of the old tractor together, her in the buddy seat next to me. She's bundled up in that navy blue coat she looks so good in, plus the pink hat and gloves I gave her for our meteor shower night.

"Ready?" I say to her, turning the key and pressing the clutch down. The engine coughs once, then catches with a low, familiar rumble.

"So ready!" The colored lights dance across her face, making her look like she belongs in some fairy tale, and I have to tear my eyes away to focus on what I'm doing.

It's been years since I've driven a tractor, but it comes back fast: clutch under my foot, hand easing the throttle forward, the steering wheel vibrating under my palms. The old Deere feels solid, familiar. I can almost hear Granddad's voice beside me, patient and gruff, teaching me when I was thirteen or fourteen: *Easy now, let her feel the road.*

I follow Isaac down the gravel drive, and then we're rolling down the shoulder of the highway, slow and steady, headed into town. In front, Maggie, Jake, and Emma are waving at us from the trailer, the dogs sitting dutifully beside them.

"So damn cute," I murmur, smiling.

"I'll say."

I glance over at Shira, expecting her to be smiling at the kids. But she's looking at me, her gaze dragging down my body with unmistakable interest.

"Like what you see?" I say, eyebrows dancing.

Her lips quirk. "Never thought I'd be turned on by a guy wearing a Santa hat, driving an ancient tractor."

"There's a first for everything, I guess." I wink.

And a last.

Dammit, I'm maudlin tonight. It's embarrassing. And ridiculous. I should be soaking this all in, not dwelling on how it's ending.

Soon we're passing the high school, the diner, all the familiar spots. It's strange—a month ago, I felt sure that things would never change here. But these past few weeks have shown me that just because things have been the same for a long time, it doesn't mean they have to *stay* the same. Even small changes make a difference. Even one person.

We've made it to the end of Main Street, and I ease off the throttle, press in the clutch, and let the old Deere roll to a stop behind Isaac and the line of decorated tractors.

I turn to Shira. "Got the candy ready?"

"Ready!" She lifts the big bag of saltwater taffy onto her lap.

"Can you turn the radio to FM 89.1?" This tractor's old enough that it didn't even have a radio when I was growing up, but Dad installed one a few years back for this very purpose. "Everyone tunes to the same station—it'll also be playing along Main Street."

Shira does, and we start rumbling forward again. The sidewalks are packed, kids sitting on the curb, families and couples and single folks, old and young, and everything in between. It's magical: the Christmas music enveloping us, twinkling lights all around, the street crowded with people.

My people, I realize. My town. I'm not sure I ever felt that way before.

"Shira!" someone calls from the street. It's a group of teenagers I've seen at the bookstore, waving at her.

She throws a handful of taffy, laughing as the kids try to catch it. Up ahead, Jake and Maggie are throwing their own candy from the trailer.

"I love this!" Shira shouts over the music at me. Her eyes are lit up, her smile huge, and that damn lump rises in my throat again.

"Me, too," I say, trying not to think about how good this all feels.

So good it hurts.

Later, after it's all over, we walk down the driveway to Shira's little cottage, hand in hand. At the door, she turns and wraps her arms around me.

"Thank you," she says, her voice muffled against my chest. "This was perfect. Just what I wanted my last night to be."

I kiss the top of her head. "Thank *you*. I loved having you be a part of everything today. You really didn't need to do that, but I—I appreciated it."

I don't know how to put it all into words—how much this has meant to me, not just today but throughout this entire holiday season. She's changed the way I think about my family, this town, and, most of all, myself.

"You probably need to head home soon, right?" she asks,

pulling back to look up at me. "Isn't everyone staying at your parents' house tonight?"

"Oh, yeah." Usually, my parents spend Christmas morning visiting the grandkids to see what Santa brought them, but since my dad's laid up, everyone's staying at my parents' house. Even Kara and Kyle are sleeping over.

"Don't you want to be there, too?" Shira asks.

"I'll go home in the morning. Unless you're sick of me?"

She shakes her head. "Not at all. I..."

"What?"

She opens her mouth, then closes it again and swallows. "Come inside. I have something for you."

"Is it you? Preferably naked?"

Shaking her head, she smiles. "Maybe later...if you can behave."

I smirk. "Come on, baby—where's the fun in that?"

Laughing, she leads me inside and into her bedroom, telling me to sit on the bed. Her suitcase is open on the floor, neatly packed. A glaring reminder that she's heading out bright and early to catch her flight. She retrieves a small box from the suitcase, then comes back over to me. It's about the size of an orange, wrapped in the same gold paper she used at the bookshop, tied with a green velvet ribbon.

I frown at her, trying to look stern. "You already got me a gift. The book—which I'm loving so far."

"Yeah, but that was for Hanukkah. This is for *Christmas*." She cocks an eyebrow. "You want it or not?"

"Gimme." I snatch it from her, unwrapping it carefully to reveal a clear glass Christmas ornament with a red ribbon at the top. And inside...

"Oh wow—it's full of little books," I say, looking closer.

She sits next to me on the bed, grinning. "They're all my

bestsellers at the shop. I know it's not as fancy as what you got me, but—"

"I love it." I stare at it, dumbfounded, wondering where she possibly could've found miniature versions of all these books. "Wait—did you *make* these?"

She gives a little shrug. "Yeah. Printed out the covers at the printshop in town, then folded them up and glued them together. It's not too difficult, just takes time."

My entire body warms at the thought of her painstakingly cutting all of these out, gluing them together. It must've taken hours. "I really, *really* love it, Shira. Thank you. So much."

After a kiss, I set the ornament down, and we lie back against her pillow, my arm around her, her head on my chest. Our legs twine together, and even though I wasn't kidding about wanting to get her naked, this is just as good. Shira tucked against me, all cozy and sweet.

My mind drifts to the inevitable: she's leaving in less than twelve hours. But it doesn't have to be the end, I tell myself. She hasn't said she wants to see me again, fine—I'll *make* her want to. We can talk on the phone, text, video call. I'll send flowers, have lunch delivered to her office, even send a damn singing telegram. Once my family no longer needs me here, I'll visit her in Chicago. Maybe Shira's not as into me as I am into her, but she's into me enough. I can work with that. I'll keep showing up until she can't help but fall the rest of the way.

I'm about to say something when she speaks.

"I've been thinking about when I was little," she says, "how sad I'd get when my favorite holidays ended, and one time I burst into tears and asked my bubbe why it couldn't be a holiday every day."

I smile at the thought of little Shira and her beloved bubbe. "What'd she say?"

"She said the holidays are special because they *don't* last forever. If every day were a holiday, none of them would stand out. Ordinary days blur together, but holidays...that's when we make the memories that stick. The ones we carry with us long after."

The words land like a stone in my chest. And then—*fuck*—my eyes start to sting. Thank God she can't see my face.

Blinking hard, I clear my throat. "Your bubbe was a wise lady."

"She really was." Her voice goes soft. "But what she said, I think it relates to the bookshop too, how it couldn't last forever, and maybe that's exactly what made it so special. I'll never forget it. I...I won't forget any of this, Jonny."

The air between us goes still. The meaning of her words settles in, without her having to say it. We're like the bookshop. We're like the holiday season itself. Brilliant for a while, unforgettable maybe—but temporary. And in that instant, I feel something inside me tear, a quiet rip only I can hear, as if whatever hope I'd been holding onto finally lets go.

"Yeah," I manage, my voice rough. "I won't forget this, either."

Desperate for something else to focus on, I lift her chin with my fingers and kiss her, slow and gentle. "Mmm, how do you always taste so sweet?" I murmur against her lips.

She laughs softly. "That's the hot cocoa we had after the parade."

"Nope, it's you. Unless you dripped hot cocoa here." I shift position so I can kiss her cheek, then her jaw. "And here." I kiss down her neck. "And here, too."

She laughs again, pulling her sweater over her head as I reach behind her and unclasp her bra. We're moving like we've done this a hundred times, like it's muscle memory—or maybe that's just me, trying to pretend that this is just another day, wishing this *could* be ordinary.

Soon we're skin to skin, my heart beating wildly. But I'm still taking my time, running my hands over every inch of her as if mapping a country I'll never visit again. Filing away each touch, each gasp, each flicker of her smile.

Trying to make it last. Keep it from fading.

Holding on tight, before it's gone.

CHAPTER 21
SHIRA
4 HOURS UNTIL MY FLIGHT LEAVES

It's still dark outside when I wake up—although does it really count as waking up if you never actually went to sleep? I closed my eyes for a while, but I was too aware of the passing time to relax. Lying in Jonny's arms, his heartbeat was a steady reminder of the ticking clock. Each pulse bringing me closer to the end of all this.

Jonny shifts beside me, and I freeze, holding my breath until his steadies. He pulls me tighter against him and mumbles something that sounds an awful lot like "stay."

And oh, how I wish I could.

I don't remember the exact moment everything changed, when I went from counting the days until I could go home to counting the days until I had to leave. But here we are on the last day, the day I was both desperate for and dreading. And there's nothing I want more than to stretch these last seconds into minutes and the minutes into hours and the hours into days. I want more days with Jonny.

But staying a few more days wouldn't change anything. I still live in Chicago. That's where my friends are, where my job is, where my life is. My real life. This was never supposed to last.

Talia would remind me that's literally the definition of a fling, which was all this was ever meant to be.

Maya always says that people come into our lives for a reason, a season, or a lifetime. And as much as I'd like to think Jonny and I could be a lifetime, I know he's either a reason or a season. The reason: making me see myself in a whole new light. And if it's a season, well, that's coming to an end, too.

Jonny starts snoring again, a soft whistle on the inhale and a tiny puff on the exhale. The sound makes me smile—everything about this man makes me smile and conjures up so many little moments. How can we have so many memories when we've only spent four weeks together? How can I feel so much, feel so different, after just a month?

Once I'm sure he's asleep, I lift his arm and slide out, placing it gently back on the bed. Jonny makes another sound, this one like a laugh. I wish I could crawl inside his mind and see what movie is playing in his dreams. One of us? Or of a Christmas morning past?

It's officially Christmas morning, I realize. The day people literally use as a metaphor for how happy someone looks, like a kid on Christmas morning.

I want Jonny to have that kind of holiday, not one that starts with me making him sad. The best gift I can give him now is trying to stave off a little of that sadness. Besides, we said everything we needed to say last night—there's no reason to draw things out with a tearful goodbye.

By some small miracle, I'm able to get dressed, zip up my suitcase, and carry it all outside without waking Jonny up. I take out the trash and leave the keys on the counter, hoping the Petersons won't mind that I didn't strip the bed. The last thing I do is kiss the note I left on my pillow for Jonny.

Hopefully, he'll understand that it was better for me to leave this way. If it came down to me actually driving away from him, I'm not sure I'd be able to do it.

It's nearly seven a.m. by the time I'm on the road. The streets are all empty; I'm the only person in Azalea who's out this early.

Instead of turning right to head out of town, I find myself turning left, toward the Christmas market. Out of habit, maybe. Or more likely, out of a sadistic need to put myself through the long goodbye I saved Jonny from.

I pass the taqueria where Jonny McKay, the town trouble-maker, first crossed my path.

I pass the restaurant where he took me out for dinner, and the Dairy Queen where we went for ice cream.

I pass the town square, where I tried to cover up the fact that I'm a Jewish girl who doesn't know all the Christmas songs. The same town square where Jonny built me a giant menorah from scrap materials to help make me feel at home, and reminded me of how and why I'm so proud to be who I am.

I pass Main Street, where just last night I got to experience my first ever tractor holiday parade, which was its own kind of magic—pure holiday joy.

And finally, I come up to the holiday market. Or now, I guess, the old textile mill. Without the stores inside, without all the books and goods and holiday treats, it's just a building. Four walls that hold nothing but the ghosts of memories.

It's sad, but inevitable. Every book has a last chapter, a last page. It all comes to a point where the only two words left to say are: *The end.* And I suppose this is that moment for the old mill. And for my Azalea story.

. . .

Two hours later, I've dropped off the rental car, and the shuttle bus has dropped me off at the Dallas Love Field airport. The terminal is eerily quiet; there isn't even a line to check my bags.

It's a good thing, and yet...

I'm about to roll up to the counter when my phone rings. Jonny's face appears on the screen, a picture of him from last night in the tractor, wearing a Santa hat and goofy grin. It rings, and rings, and rings. I hold my breath, waiting for it to go to voicemail.

I can't handle talking to him right now. He's going to be mad. Or worse, hurt. But with some distance, hopefully, he'll understand that I made the best decision. For him, if not for me.

The ringing stops only to start again, and my eyes fill with tears looking at Jonny's smiling, happy photo, knowing that on the other end, he's anything but.

It rings again, and a few tears escape, salty tracks sliding down my cheeks. I still can't talk to him. Not now. Not yet.

But there is someone I can talk to—and since it's after nine a.m., she might be awake.

I roll my luggage over to the Starbucks and sink into an empty chair. Maya answers my FaceTime call on the second ring.

"Merry Christmas," she says in a sleepy, sing-song voice. She's sitting up in bed, her hair in a messy bun.

"Hi," I say, my voice wobbly with emotion.

My best friend's face falls as she takes in the sight of me. "What's wrong? What did that asshole with the big magic dick do?"

"Nothing," I manage to croak out. "If anything, I'm the asshole."

I tell Maya about last night and this morning, my decision to leave without saying goodbye, and how I'm now wondering if that was the right thing to do.

"It was kind of a dick move," she agrees.

"I know, but I couldn't," I say, sniffing. "Saying goodbye would have been too hard."

"Babe, you can't skip past the hard things—you really have feelings for this guy, don't you?"

That's all it takes for the tears I've been holding back to finally fall. "I know it was just supposed to be a fling, but..."

"Shira, sweetie, we encouraged you to have a fling because we wanted you to put yourself out there. We didn't want you to sit at home moping all day, waiting for the month to be over. We wanted you to turn this shitty situation into an opportunity—and that's exactly what you did. It's okay if Jonny's more than a fling. I'm proud of you for being brave and going for it with him!"

"I know, but that's part of the problem," I say. "The way I've been with him—I've never acted like this before. It felt real, but what if this is just some version I made up?"

"Or what if this *is* the real you? The you that's been there all along, hidden under layers of trying to be what everyone else expects. Maybe Jonny's the first person who's made you feel safe enough to let her show."

A few tears slip down my cheeks. "I don't know."

"Why don't you change your flight?" she suggests. "Stay a few more days."

"I can't."

"Why not?"

"Because," I say, sounding like a petulant child.

"Because why?" Maya says defiantly. I should know better than to act immature with a woman who spends all day teaching third graders.

"Because I have plans tonight—with you," I remind her. "And I've missed all our other holiday traditions this year."

"Shira, I love you, but we can get Chinese food and watch a movie literally any other night."

"But I don't want to disappear like Anya did," I say, the tears falling even faster.

"Wait, what?" she asks. "What does Anya have to do with anything?"

"She got her happy ending, and it doesn't include us. She moved ten miles away, and it's like she doesn't exist. I don't want that to happen to me—first you fall off the group text, and then you fall out of the friend group, and then..."

"Babe," Maya says, her voice firm. "First, you aren't Anya. Second, relationships take work—even friendships. And no matter where you are or who you're with, you aren't going to lose us. And I don't think we lost Anya, either. She's just in a season of her life where she doesn't have time for us. But when she does..."

"We'll let her back in the group chat?" I ask, wiping my tears with the back of my hand.

"If she wants," she says. "Although I'm not sure she'll love getting three hundred alerts a day about the shenanigans her single friends from college are getting into."

"I really don't like change," I admit.

"I get it," Maya says. "It can be scary—but it's also how we grow. Look at you, Shir. You've changed so much over this last month. You're more confident and comfortable with who you are—who is amazing, by the way."

"I do think this has been good for me," I admit.

"So are you going to stay?"

"I don't think I can," I say, new tears stinging my eyes. "He's probably mad at me because of this morning. And I really don't want to miss our tradition tonight—I've missed you guys so much. And I have to get back for work, anyway."

"Not until Monday," Maya says. "That's five days away. If I

had the option of letting a hot man who is literally obsessed with me bone me for five more nights—I'd take that over cold crab rangoon any day."

"He's not obsessed."

She fixes me with a stern look. "Shira Schwartz, the man built you a giant menorah and had the town—where you were the only Jew—throw you a Hanukkah party."

I sigh, thinking back to that night, and the shock and surprise of turning around the corner. The realization that it wasn't a Christmas carol they were singing, but a Hanukkah version they sang just for me. I push the thought away.

"Yeah, but I have to get ready for my meeting with Conor—he wants a presentation on everything I learned being 'boots on the ground.'"

"And what did you learn?" Maya asks.

"I haven't started making the PowerPoint yet."

"Fuck the PowerPoint. What did you learn?"

"I don't know," I say.

"Bullshit," Maya says, never one for mincing words. "Tell me one thing you learned."

I shake my head, thinking maybe I would have been better off if I'd answered Jonny's call instead of calling Maya.

"I learned that stories have the power to change people's lives; that working ten hours a day on my feet is exhausting, but it's totally worth it when you've helped a person find their next favorite book." My throat tightens as I think about all the different people I got to know in Azalea, how grateful they were for the bookshop. "I learned that it's never too early, or too late, to become a reader. That sometimes, people just want to talk to someone about a book they read. And that I...."

"You what?"

That maybe I can belong somewhere I never expected to.

The thought hits me like a lightning bolt, and I quickly shove it away, terrified of what it might mean.

"Conor doesn't want to hear any of that," I say, shaking my head. "He'll want to know about the ROI, the demographics, and the cost-benefit analysis."

She lets out an exaggerated yawn. "Boring."

"So is the job."

"Exactly!" Maya shouts so loud that I lower the volume on my headphones. "You only want the promotion because you want to prove that you can get it. You want the validation even though your asshole boss couldn't see a good thing if it slapped him in the face."

She's right. I took this job because it was the only one I could get after graduating from college. I stayed because I was good at it, and a job was a job. And, yes, of course, I wanted my boss to recognize my value and worth.

"It's not like I can just quit," I say. "I need to pay rent. And I don't know what else I would want to do—even if I wanted to stay in Azalea, the market is gone. The bookstore is gone. Even Jonny is going to be gone soon."

"Okay," Maya says, which is not helpful in the slightest.

"Okay?" I repeat, my voice rising in frustration. "What am I supposed to do with that?"

"Come home," she says, shrugging. "We'll hug your brains out, eat so much Chinese food that it will make our bellies hurt until we're hungry two hours later, and watch cheesy, unrealistic rom-coms."

"And then what?" I ask, my voice small.

"And then we'll figure it out. You can always go back—there's got to be at least a dozen flights between Dallas and Chicago every day. Or he could come here to visit—you said he's leaving soon anyway, right?"

"Right," I say, but it all feels wrong.

"You're going to be okay, Shir," Maya says. "It's all going to be okay."

"I hope you're right."

"I'm always right," she says. "I'm a teacher."

That gets a laugh out of me. "True."

"Safe travels, babe—we'll see you soon."

I hang up and dry my eyes, then sit for a moment, thinking back to something Maya said.

What if this is you? The you that's been there all along, just hidden under layers of trying to be what everyone else expects. And Jonny's the first person who's made you feel safe enough to let her show.

I think that's the real lesson I learned running the bookshop —that we're drawn to books because every one of us holds a multitude of stories. And just like you can't judge a book by its cover, you can't judge a person. Or a town.

At the end of the day, we're not just the main character of our own story, but we have a role to play in the stories of everyone whose path we cross. If we're brave, we can discover a whole new side of ourselves. But when we hide or shrink ourselves down to what we think other people want, we rob the world of something beautiful. The person we have the potential to be and all the stories we have left to live.

If I go back to my old life and pretend like none of this changed me, it'll be like closing the book before the ending. I'll never know how the story could've gone. And I'd regret that for the rest of my life.

I stand, heart pounding with the kind of reckless hope I've been too scared to allow. I've spent so long being careful, fitting in, bending to other people's expectations. What if I chose something for *myself*? Where *I* want to belong. Who *I* want to be.

And in that moment, I know what I have to do. I need to call on all the bravery and boldness I've been practicing this month. Hopefully, I'm not too late.

CHAPTER 22

JONNY

SHE'S GONE

When I step in my parents' front door, Christmas morning hits me like a tidal wave of noise and color. Kids in matching pajamas race between piles of wrapping paper, Bing Crosby croons in the background, and the scent of baking cinnamon rolls fills the air.

It should feel warm and comforting—this is my favorite day of the year. Instead, I'm numb. My mind keeps replaying how it felt to wake up alone. To find a note on my pillow saying *Thanks for a beautiful December.* To call and call and get no response. To realize that she left without saying goodbye.

That she's gone.

"Uncle Jonny!" Emma shrieks when she spots me, and then all the nieces and nephews are swarming me, hands tugging at mine, voices overlapping as they tell me what Santa brought them. I try to smile, but my face feels weird, and I'm not sure it's working.

"Hey, kids," Annabel says gently, stepping in. "Let's give Uncle Jonny a second, okay?"

I blink at her. She looks worried. Actually, everyone does.

My mom is perched on the arm of Dad's recliner, fingers laced with his. Kara's on the couch, Kyle standing behind her. Bianca and Chad sit on the floor amid torn wrapping paper. Every single one of them is watching me.

My brother comes up and puts a hand on my shoulder. "You good, man?"

"It's Christmas morning." I manage a shrug. "Why wouldn't I be good?"

Isaac studies me for a second. "Yeah," he says finally.

Mom catches my eye across the room, her expression full of concern. "Jonny...?"

"Keep unwrapping," I say, shaking my head. "I'll be right back."

I make it to the kitchen doorway and stop, pressing my palm to the doorframe like it's the only thing holding me up. Then I squeeze my eyes shut and try to breathe.

I'm fine. It's fine. Shira's gone, and it's completely, absolutely, fucking *fine*.

"You're moping."

I turn to see Bianca a few feet away, watching me. "No, I'm not."

She nods. "Like the time in eighth grade when you got grounded for stealing lip gloss for that girl you liked."

"Just need a cup of coffee," I mutter.

"Shira left this morning?" Chad says as he comes over to stand next to his wife, and I nod. "Are y'all going to see each other again?"

Twenty-four hours ago, I would've bet on it—some kind of future, however complicated, waiting for us to figure it out. But now? Feels like she already gave me her answer, and I'd be an idiot not to take the hint.

So I shrug. "Probably not."

"Wait, you just let her leave?" Bianca asks, sounding incredulous.

Not really up to me. My jaw clenches, and my voice comes out flat: "Drop it, B."

Of course, I know damn well she's not going to drop it. She's studying me with her eyes narrowed, like she's mentally drafting the longest sisterly lecture of all time. Over in the living room, the kids have gone back to playing with their toys, but the adults have all stopped their conversation, watching us while trying to look like they're not.

Bianca sighs, shaking her head. "Well, it was bound to happen anyway. I heard she was dating someone back in Chicago, but he wanted to take a break when she came here."

I glare at her. "And you're telling me this now because...?"

"Because she's probably going to get back together with him once she gets home."

It's like a bucket of ice hits me. "The fuck? Are you serious?"

She shrugs. "That's what I heard."

The room tilts. All of a sudden, it makes a horrible kind of sense—this really was just an interlude for her, a vacation from her real life. I can see it in my mind: Shira rolling her bags through Midway Airport, coming outside to see some guy waiting at arrivals. Some fucking asshole moron who clearly doesn't deserve her, because why would anyone want a "break" from a woman like her? I imagine her eyes lighting up when she spots him, those big brown eyes I already miss so much it hurts, and my stomach bottoms out. Jealousy, devastation, regret—it all crashes into me so hard I almost choke.

"That can't—I can't—you've got to be fucking kidding me." My voice cracks on the last word.

I'm breathing too fast, chest heaving. I can't stop imagining it: Shira running to him, putting her arms around him. Kissing him. And then my brain decides to really torture me as it jumps forward through the years. Wedding dress. Picket fence. Babies.

I want to throw up. Or punch a hole in the wall. Or both.

I'm not sure who I hate more—this nameless, faceless guy, or myself. Because *I'm* the fucking asshole moron. I let her leave. I let her slip out of my hands, and now she's going to slip right back into his.

"I'm kidding, Jonny," Bianca says softly.

The words barely register. The entire room is a blur, and my heart's a jackhammer against my ribs. "What?"

"I'm kidding," she repeats. "But you should've seen your face."

The details of the room slide back into focus: the Christmas tree, wrapping paper all over the floor, and my older sister smirking like we're kids again, and she just ate my dessert.

I lunge toward her, forgetting momentarily that I've got six inches and more than fifty pounds on her—

"Whoa there," Chad says, stepping between us with his hand on my chest. "That's my wife. Back off."

I stop instantly, breathing hard; of course, I'm not going to tackle her. Even if I really, *really* want to.

"You're my least favorite sister," I growl, pointing at her.

Over from the couch, Kara pumps her fist. "*Yes!*"

"And you..." Chad turns to Bianca. "I love you, but that was a shitty thing to do."

She puts a hand on her hip, staring straight at me. "Or was it brilliant? Because you know how you feel about her now, right?"

I pause, running a hand down my face. *How do I feel?*

Well, my ribs feel like they've splintered. My heart feels like it's bruised all over. My eyes are stinging, my stomach is churning, and my throat is so tight and swollen I'm not sure I could force a single word out.

When I look up again, Bianca's staring at me, her face softening. "Oh. You're in love with her," she whispers, almost like she can't believe it herself.

I swallow past the thick lump in my throat, forcing out the truth I've been avoiding for days. "Yeah."

My mother gasps softly.

The room goes quiet, then Annabel stands and says, "Does she know that?"

I shake my head.

"The question is," Isaac says, putting an arm around his wife, "what are you going to do about it?"

I look past them at the rest of the room. My mom and sisters have tears in their eyes, Kyle and Chad are giving me nods of solidarity, and Dad's just stroking his beard, as if he knew it all along. Even the little kids are watching. My family: loud, messy, chaotic, but mine. For so long, I've felt like the odd one out, but the truth is, they've been in my corner all along. Maybe they don't fully understand me, and they sure as shit won't ever stop teasing me...but they love me unconditionally. Always have. Just took a few weeks of actually sticking around for me to recognize it.

Taking a deep breath, I straighten up. "I need to talk to her. Face to face, before she leaves. Just hope I can get there in time."

Isaac nods, satisfied.

"Well, start movin'," Dad booms from his recliner. "You're burnin' daylight, for God's sake."

Bianca opens her mouth, ready to scold Dad for language, then sighs and holds up her hand before I can even state the obvious.

"I know," she says, then smiles at me. "Go get your girl."

· · ·

The entire way to the airport, I drive twenty over the speed limit, hands white-knuckled on the steering wheel. There's no traffic, thank Christ (literally, thank you baby Jesus and everyone celebrating your birth by staying the fuck home), and I'm sending up frantic prayers that I don't blow past some highway patrolman who's got a chip on his shoulder because he got stuck working Christmas morning. Please, God, Santa, whoever's on shift up there—just let me make it in time.

My eyes keep jerking to the clock on the dash, watching the minutes flick by. She had to return the rental car, then she'll have to check her bags. Hopefully, I'll catch her before she goes through security, but even if I don't, I have a plan B: buy a ticket on her flight. Or the next one after that, or the next one after that.

And if all else fails, I've got a plan C: charter a goddamn plane to Chicago.

Finally, I pull up to the departures area of the terminal and screech to a stop, not even bothering with short-term parking. Hardly anyone's around, and what's the worst that can happen? The truck gets impounded? I'll deal with that later.

I hop out of the truck and slam the door shut, heading for the automatic doors—

"Jonny!"

I turn. And there she is, about thirty yards down the empty sidewalk with her suitcase, just outside another set of automatic doors.

"Shira?" I call, starting in her direction.

"What the hell are you doing here?" she shouts back.

Probably not the ideal response, given what I'm planning to say to her, but I remind myself that it doesn't matter. All I want is a chance to tell her how I feel. She can decide what she wants to do with it.

"I need to talk to you," I say, my heart rate quickening as I get closer. "Last night? What you said about how holidays can't last forever, or they won't be special?"

She nods, confused.

I stop about six feet away from her. "That's bullshit."

It comes out sharper than I mean, and her eyebrows jump. Guess I'm not winning any awards for romantic speeches this morning.

"I mean, yeah, maybe it's true for holidays," I continue, stumbling over my words, "but some things *can* last and still be special. Like—like take the bookshop, for example. If it was always there, it wouldn't lose its magic, it would become even more embedded in the town. Sure, over time people would get used to it, but that doesn't mean anyone would take it for granted. Knowing that something's always there, that you can count on it, that it's woven into everyday life—" I swallow hard. "That shouldn't make it less special. It should make you love it even *more.*"

She stares at me for a second before speaking. "You came all this way to talk to me about the bookstore?"

"No—I mean, yes, but that's not—" I take another step closer. My heart is hammering again. "I don't want the bookstore to end, but mostly...I don't want *us* to end. We're so good together, Shira. And I think that if we had more time, we would be even better, but we won't know unless we try. I need to stay in Azalea for a few more weeks, but after that, I can go anywhere. And okay, maybe it is kind of insane to fall in love so quickly, but—"

"Wait, what?"

Her voice is a hoarse whisper. And that's when I notice her eyes are all shiny and red. She's crying. Actually, it looks like she's been crying for a while.

I shift my weight, not sure if this is good or bad.

"I've never felt anything like this before," I say, quieter. "And it's not just because I forced myself to slow down for the first time, it's you. The way you pulled me out of the hamster wheel I've been on for so long. The way you quietly connect with people, noticing and appreciating them for their unique selves. The way you shared yourself with me and somehow saw parts of me I didn't even know were there. Most of all...it's the way you make me feel, Shira. You've got me wanting things I've never wanted before, like permanence. You make me want to create something that'll stand the test of time, a life I'll never stop working to make stronger and better."

I swallow, centering myself.

"I don't want to look back and realize that I let something precious slip through my fingers because I wasn't brave enough to say how I felt out loud. You don't need to say anything back, I just couldn't let you go without making sure you know."

I take one final step until we're a foot apart, and she tilts her chin up, those beautiful brown eyes searching mine.

"Shira, I'm falling in love with you," I say, my voice steady now. "And I want the chance to love you even more."

Her bottom lip starts to quiver. Her eyes flood with tears. And then she goes up on tiptoe and kisses me.

The world around us fades. Nothing exists except her lips on mine. Nothing matters but the fact that she's kissing me.

She's kissing me.

Shira is kissing me, and everything is perfect.

"Jonny," she says, a little breathless as she pulls away. "Do you remember what time my flight leaves?"

My mind is a blur, but I do remember that. "Ten forty-five."

"And what time is it?"

Taking a step back, I glance at my watch. 10:22. "Shit, you haven't even checked your bags, you're going to miss—"

"Shhh," She puts a hand on my cheek, tipping my face gently down to meet her eyes again. "I was trying to call an

Uber, but there aren't many driving right now. I was starting to panic."

I stare at her. "You were…"

"Heading back to Azalea. To *you.*"

"Why?"

She throws up her hands. "Why do you think, you big idiot? Because you aren't the only one who's falling in love."

My heart stops.

"You're serious?" I whisper. "Because it would be really mean to joke about that right now."

She's smiling, tears on her lashes. "I think that's the only explanation for how completely out of character I've been acting."

My entire body floods with relief and elation. And then I step forward and wrap my arms around her waist and lift her, spinning her slowly as her words sink in. It feels like a miracle.

"Hey!" someone shouts.

I look up to see a man wearing a Santa hat and a reflective vest, standing by my dad's truck, waving at me.

"This your vehicle?" he shouts.

I set Shira down gently. "Yes, sir!" I call. "Coming back right now."

"Well, hurry on up," he says, shaking his head as he walks away.

Shira smirks at me. "Troublemaker."

"Me? How am *I* the troublemaker when you're the one who snuck out this morning without saying goodbye?"

Her eyes immediately turn sad. "I'm sorry I wasn't brave enough to say goodbye—I didn't want to go."

I press a kiss to the top of her head. "I will most likely forgive you. But it wouldn't hurt if you tried to make it up to me tonight in creative ways."

"Oh yeah?" Her eyes sparkle. "And what would that entail?"

"You know what, don't worry about it," I tell her, grabbing the handle of her suitcase. "You can just lie back and watch a pro work."

Grinning, she rolls her eyes. "You are so full of yourself."

"Full of *myself*?" I smirk. "Babe, you're about to be full of me."

"Is that a threat or a promise?"

I lean in, voice dropping. "Depends on how good you are at following directions."

Her cheeks flush bright red, and I take her hand, lacing our fingers together, then start heading back to the truck.

"So," she says casually, "speaking of permanence...I hear there's an old textile factory for sale back in Azalea that might be perfect for a bookstore."

"Not anymore."

She blinks. "What?"

"It's not for sale. I bought it."

"Jonny McKay!" She smacks my shoulder. "Were you going to share that information?"

"It was on the list, right after 'tell Shira she's the love of my life,' but then you kissed me, and I got a little distracted by all the joy."

She's shaking her head, smiling, as we start walking again. "Does that mean you're moving back for good?"

"I haven't figured that out yet," I say. "Right now, I'm just thinking about building something that can last."

"I love that," she says, smiling. "What do you think about putting a real bookstore in the textile mill? One with built-in bookcases and a reading nook—"

"And a coffee counter?" I add.

"And maybe some other shops—"

"And what about apartments on the top floor?"

We're talking over each other, and we both laugh.

"Guess we'd better start drafting a business plan," I say, smiling down at her. My heart is swelling with pride and love, and so much excitement for the future that it could burst right out of my chest.

She smiles up at me, bright-eyed. "Later, Jonny. Right now, you need to take me home for Christmas."

EPILOGUE

JONNY

Two years later

It's Christmas Eve and the first night of Hanukkah, one of those rare times when the two holidays overlap, and I'm headed to Azalea with Shira.

"You feeling okay, love?" I ask, looking over at her in the passenger seat.

She's seemed tense this whole drive, but the closer we get, the more her knee bounces. "Yeah. I'm good," she says.

I lace my fingers with hers, hoping to ease her nerves. It's our third time doing Hanukkah and Christmas celebrations in Azalea, but I guess this year is a little different, now that we're co-owners of Azalea's newest business venture.

"I'll be right by your side," I say, lifting her hand and pressing it to my lips. "Always."

She takes a deep breath. "I know."

The diamond ring burning a hole in my pocket will hopefully make that "always" official. *Mine.* The word that started as a quiet hope two years ago, a whispered wish to the universe that somehow, miraculously, came true.

It's been a wild ride to get here, compared to that Christmas morning when I raced to the airport with no plan except to tell her how I felt. At first, everything between us was shiny, exciting...and complicated. She stayed in Azalea for a few extra days before heading back to Chicago, and I spent the next several weeks ping-ponging between my parents' house and her apartment.

Traveling back and forth was exhausting, but it was worth it. Our time together was magical, getting to know each other better, driving each other crazy in the bedroom—then staying up late sketching renovation ideas and dreaming bigger than either of us would've dared alone. Falling in love a little more every day.

Shira was hesitant to just up and quit her job, which I understood, especially since Conor finally gave her that long-deserved promotion. But by December of last year, we knew our relationship was solid, and it was clear the renovation needed our full attention. So she quit.

By then, I was practically living in her apartment and flying to Texas every couple of weeks, which wasn't sustainable. That's when the real question hit: where should we settle? We were both ready to put down roots somewhere, but as much as we love Azalea, we're city people at heart. Dallas ended up being the perfect spot—it has a thriving Jewish community, and it's close enough to Azalea while also giving us our own space. The best of both worlds.

Waking up next to Shira every morning never gets old—even though she steals the covers, puts way too many throw pillows on the couch, and leaves strands of her hair all over.

And now, I'm so excited to ask her to marry me, I can hardly drive straight. It shouldn't be a total surprise to her—hell, I started dropping hints six months after we met, until she flat-out told me to slow the fuck down. She said she wanted to live together for at least a year before getting engaged. She also reminded me that the anticipation is part of the magic. But that one-year mark passed last week, and I'm not about to wait any longer to put a ring on it.

"Can we stop by the bookstore on the way?" Shira asks as we head through town.

I glance over at her. "It's almost sundown."

"I'll make it quick." Her eyes go wide. "Please?"

"Of course." I give her hand another squeeze. "You sure you're okay?"

She nods, but she looks pale, and now *I'm* a little nervous. Did she somehow figure out what I'm planning?

My shoulders tense as I turn into the parking lot of the textile factory, now renamed The Old Mill. The grand opening was on December 1st, and it's been non-stop busy ever since. As we enter the building, a wave of satisfaction hits me, even though everything is closed now. We did it; we created the dream we started brainstorming on our way home from the airport on Christmas Day, two years ago. There's no way I could've done it without Shira. She likes to say we were equal partners, but all I did was put up the money. She brought all the magic.

The bookstore sits at the heart of the main floor, flanked by several permanent shops for local businesses, with a few other spaces that rotate seasonally, as well as office space on the second floor and condos on the third. Shira has been an essential partner in all of it, but the bookstore is her special project. She personally designed the layout, hired every bookseller, and hand-selected the stock. She makes the drive up several times a week, connecting with customers and making sure everything is perfect.

We named it *The Book Haven*, and that's exactly what it's become. More than just a place to buy books—though plenty of that happened this month—it's a hub of life and laughter. Parents bring their kids for story time, a group of older ladies meets every Sunday afternoon for coffee and conversation, and teenagers swing by after school to hang out. It's alive in a way I never imagined, already essential to the town, and I can't wait to watch it flourish even more in the years to come.

"Hey there," a voice calls, and I look up to see Alan Larson moseying through the hall. He and his wife opened a stationary and candle shop two doors down from the bookstore. "Congrats on all the success! It's been a good opening month. Always knew you had it in you."

"Thanks," I say, smiling. The people of Azalea have surprised me with their support. Shira says all I had to do was give them the chance to get to know the new me, but I'm pretty sure they only put up with me because they adore her.

"I'll be right back," Shira says, giving me a brief smile. "I just need to wrap a gift."

After she disappears into the bookstore, I chat with Mr. Larson about a few ideas he has for increasing foot traffic at The Mill, until Shira calls for me. "Jonny, can you come in here?"

I head into the darkened shop, where she's standing by the register with a wrapped gift in her hands, chewing on her bottom lip.

"Here," she says, thrusting the box at me.

I glance at her, eyebrows raised. "But...we're doing presents tonight and tomorrow morning, right?"

"I want you to open this one now. Please?"

Still confused, I take the package from her. It's wrapped in gold paper and tied with a white velvet ribbon. "Fancy," I murmur.

"Don't you dare drag this out," she warns.

I slowly slide my finger under a taped edge, teasing her, until I see how nervous she looks. Then my stomach knots up. I rip off the paper, open the box, and—

My heart stops beating.

Two books I recognize from the bookstore's children's section are nestled inside: *Baby's First Hanukkah. Baby's First Christmas.*

My heart slams back into rhythm, hard and fast. I can't move, can't speak. Can hardly breathe.

"Jonny?"

Shira's voice cuts through the daze, soft and trembling.

"A baby?" I whisper, looking at her.

She's standing there with her hands knotted together. "I— I've been kind of tired but I assumed it was just the stress of the store opening, but then I realized I'd missed my period a while back, so I took a test this morning and...and it was positive." One hand lightly goes to her lower belly. "I couldn't wait another minute without you knowing, too. I know we didn't plan for this yet, but it happened, and I hope—"

I scoop her into my arms, lifting her off her feet. She lets out a startled yelp as I spin her around.

When I set her down, I stare at her, still stunned. "A *baby?*"

"Is that...okay?" Her expression is half-nervous, half-hopeful.

My plans for later go out the window. I drop to my knees in front of her, hands shaking so hard I can barely get the ring box out of my pocket. Taking a steadying breath, I flip it open and look up at her. She's gazing down at me, eyes wide, lips parted.

"I was going to do this tonight," I say, "but I can't think of a better time and place than right here, right now. Because as we know, sometimes life gives you exactly what you need before you even realize you're ready, right?"

She nods, letting out a shaky exhale.

"I had a whole speech planned," I admit, "but I forgot every word of it. So you'll have to trust me that it was going to be epic."

That earns a watery laugh, and her eyes fill with tears.

I exhale, trying to find the right words. "It's kind of perfect that the first time I saw you was on Thanksgiving, because you give me a new reason to be thankful every single day. Shira, you're my favorite person on the planet. You've shown me how it feels to be truly loved. You've made me want to plant some roots and grow into someone better than I've been. And now you're growing my second favorite person on the planet—half you, half me, though hopefully mostly you."

She lets out another soft laugh as a few tears roll down her cheeks.

I swallow, my own eyes stinging. "Shira Schwartz, love of my life, will you marry me?"

Now Shira's crying too hard to speak, but she's nodding, and then we're kissing, and as I pull her close, it hits me: I'm holding my entire world in my arms. Our own little family.

I could've stayed wrapped up with Shira in our own little bubble for the next few hours, but we have places to go and people to see. We arrive at the town square a few minutes after sundown, a little late, but we both needed a moment to regroup. Shira's nerves have melted away, replaced by a radiant smile that shines like the diamond ring on her finger.

People greet her everywhere we go—handshakes, hugs, cheerful hellos—and I'm so proud my chest might burst. Never in my life have I felt this lucky.

The town square is packed. Last year, word of the giant menorah got out, and a few Jewish people in the area came. Tonight, it looks like there are even more. It feels extra special because the two holidays are colliding, bringing together different communities that might not usually overlap. The menorah I built two years ago stands proudly at one end, the "candles" ready to be illuminated, and the big Christmas tree sparkles at the other. Strings of lights crisscross overhead, and tables are set up in the center, filled with tamales and latkes, hot cocoa and coffee, sufganiyot and gingerbread cookies.

Shira sucks in a breath. "Wait—is that...?"

Her friends, Maya, Talia, and Naomi, are standing over by the menorah. The moment they spot her, they start running toward us. They surround her, hugging, shrieking, and laughing.

Shira looks at me, stunned. "Did you do this?"

"He flew us out here first class, rented us a Mercedes, and got us a swanky hotel room in Dallas," Maya says.

Talia nods. "So it was kind of hard to say no."

"And we couldn't miss the chance to visit you!" Naomi adds.

"I want them to see everything you've created here," I tell Shira. "All your work, all the magic you poured into the bookstore...and into this town."

My original plan was to propose in front of friends and family later tonight. I want her to see that I'm committed to blending our lives, our traditions, and the people we love. Carving out a space where we both belong, separately and together. It matters even more now, with a baby—*our baby!*—on the way.

"Girl!" Talia suddenly shouts. "What is on your finger?"

Shira beams, holding up her left hand. "I'm engaged!"

Her friends shriek and hug her, jumping up and down with excitement. Then they're hugging me, too, telling me I crushed it with the ring (I just followed their secret instructions from a few months ago: make it stunningly gorgeous but not too huge).

Then Shira comes up next to me. "Can I tell them our other news?" she whispers in my ear. "But no one else yet. Is that okay?"

"Of course."

I kiss her forehead before letting go, and she faces her friends, balling her hands into fists as she takes a deep breath.

"And also....I'm pregnant!" Shira whisper-shrieks.

And then they're all screaming again, hugging and jumping and cheering as I watch, smiling.

"We're going to be aunts!" Maya says, brushing tears from her eyes.

"And bridesmaids!" Naomi adds.

"What was that?"

Turning, I see my mom standing behind me, eyes lit up with barely concealed hope.

I hesitate, not wanting to spill anything that Shira isn't ready to share, but she's already nudging me with a grin. "You can tell her everything," she says.

So I put my arm around my mom and lean in. "We're getting married, and we're having a baby," I say quietly. "But no one else needs to know that second part yet, okay?"

Of course, she immediately bursts into tears. "I won't tell a soul," she promises, nodding furiously.

Because sure, no one's going to wonder at all why she's ugly crying in the town square. And of course, that's when I spot my older sister walking up with her husband and kids. I groan internally.

"Mom?" Bianca asks, alarmed. "What's wrong?"

"Nothing," Mom says, sniffing and wiping her eyes. "I'm just so happy Jonny and Shira are...here."

Bianca turns to me, eyes narrowing. "What did you do?"

I lift my hands. "Nothing!"

Kara and Kyle arrive, their toddler in the stroller, followed by Isaac and Annabel with their three kids in tow. Then finally, Dad ambles over, carrying the cane the physical therapist wishes he would actually use.

"Jonny," Kara says, pointing a finger at me, "what did you do?"

"Why does everyone immediately assume it's me?" I demand.

"Because Mom is crying and you're standing there looking guilty," Isaac says.

"I don't look guilty!"

"You look like you just raided the cookie jar," Bianca says, and her husband nods.

"Out with it, son," Dad says sternly to me. "What is going on here?"

Mom sniffles and buries her face in his chest, which doesn't help my case at all.

"It's nothing bad," I say, looking around at everyone.

"Well, you made your mama cry," Isaac says, smirking now. "So, either you screwed up...or you finally did something right."

"Oh, just tell them," Shira says, laughing.

I sigh. "Fine, all you meddling McKays! We're engaged, and Shira is pregnant. Happy now?"

There's a beat of stunned silence—and then absolute chaos. Everyone is shouting, cheering, kids jumping around, my sisters grabbing Shira's hand to look at the ring and squealing loud enough to be heard in the next county. Isaac slaps me on the back, Dad lets out a booming laugh, and Mom is full-on sobbing.

When everyone's done celebrating, we introduce my family to Shira's friends, and then it's time for the third annual lighting of the Azalea menorah, followed by the tractor parade.

But before that starts, I take a moment to wrap my arms around Shira, letting the sights and sounds of the square wash over me. The twinkling lights, the laughter, the warm scent of cinnamon and cocoa, the glow of the menorah and the Christmas tree—it feels like a rare, quiet kind of magic. A reminder that sharing our traditions is one way to see each other more fully, honor the ways we're different, and recognize all the many threads that connect us. Maybe we can't solve every problem in the world, but in these small, shared moments, we can do just a little bit better.

This is home, I realize, as Shira leans into me. Not a place on a map, but right here with the people we love: the family I was born into, the family Shira chose along the way, and the family we're beginning to grow. All of us, together, finding our way through this messy, beautiful life. Right where we belong.

———

ACKNOWLEDGMENTS

The idea for this story began this summer, at a bookstore we visited on tour with our latest novel, *Battle of the Bookstores*. We arrived at The Reading Rabbit in Azle, Texas a half-hour late due to a delayed flight—a little flustered and unsure of what to expect. We were instantly welcomed by a shop full of enthusiastic readers who made us feel right at home. As we signed books, we kept hearing the same thing from people: even though the store had only been open a few months, it had already had a huge impact on their lives and their town.

That night, we couldn't stop thinking about the difference a bookstore can make in a community. As lifelong readers and lovers of indie bookshops ourselves, we know how true this is. That night, we started brainstorming a story about a town that had never had a bookstore and realized it was the perfect setup for a holiday novella. Thank you to Momma Rabbit (Vicki Rhodus) and Papa Rabbit (Ronnie Rhodus), Mikayla Mitchell, and the entire crew at The Reading Rabbit for inviting us to your store—and for the gift baskets that included dilly beans (which were so delicious they made it into the story!).

While the idea was sparked by one specific bookstore, we've had similar interactions at other indie bookstores across the country, where we've seen first-hand how important bookstores are to a community. Thank you to all the booksellers who work tirelessly to connect readers and authors, create safe spaces for readers, and open hearts and minds through books. We're so grateful for your support of us and our books!

Huge thanks to our incredible crew of beta readers: Ali Rosen, Dallas Strawn, Mary Chase, Courtney Marzilli, Paige Moreland, Debby Brauer, Jennifer Schutte, Nicole Mavrides, Allison Lilly, Vanessa Figueroa, Kaitlynn Hammond, Lauren Paletz, Hannah Rafferty, Meghan Long, and Laura Sloane. Thank you for reading on a very short timeline, for catching errors, giving feedback, and sharing details about Texas. Without you, this story wouldn't be nearly as strong—and it would have a lot more commas in the wrong places.

A few additional thank yous to Anya Corson Chotiner for the help with the Jewish brisket, Jamie Beck for the help with the legalese, Danielle Zadra for her Photoshop skills, and Nate Godfrey for his help with the details of alfalfa farming and the locky-spinny things! Also thanks to the Starbucks #22423 in Chicago for keeping Alison caffeinated and letting her camp out at her favorite table for hours and hours on end.

We'd like to thank our agents, Joanna MacKenzie and Amy Berkower, who came through big time saving us from a small clerical error... And also to the amazing Bookstagram squad who helped us announce this novella and reveal the cover.

Most of all, thank you to our readers. If we can whisk you away from the world for a few hours while you're reading one of our books, we will have succeeded. Thank you for supporting us through the years, showing up at events, recommending our books to friends, and reaching out to tell us how much our stories mean to you. We do this for you!

From our hearts to yours, we wish you a Happy Hanukkah, a Merry Christmas, and a magical holiday season!

Love,
Alison & Bradeigh
AKA Ali Brady

ABOUT THE AUTHOR

Ali Brady is the pen name of writing BFFs Alison Hammer and Bradeigh Godfrey. They are the USA TODAY Bestselling author of romantic, heartwarming, funny novels including *The Beach Trap, The Comeback Summer, Until Next Summer,* and *Battle of the Bookstores.* Their books have been "best of summer" picks by *The Washington Post, The Wall Street Journal, Parade,* and Katie Couric Media. Alison lives in Chicago and works as an advertising creative director. She's also the Founder and Co-President of The Artists Against Antisemitism, and the author of *You and Me and Us* and *Little Pieces of Me.* Bradeigh lives in Utah with her husband, four children, and two dogs. She works as a doctor and is the author of psychological thrillers *Imposter and The Followers.*

Subscribe to our newsletter to stay up to date:
www.alibradybooks.substack.com

www.ingramcontent.com/pod-product-compliance
Lightning Source LLC
Chambersburg PA
CBHW050313110726
47899CB00007B/2219